BREAKING THE WORLD

BREAKING THE WORLD

JERRY GORDON

PRAISE FOR JERRY GORDON

The things we do to each other are more awful than any haunted house, ghoul, or demon could ever be, and in BREAKING THE WORLD, Jerry Gordon delivers an unflinching look at real-life horror. This novel will gnaw its way through your skull, burrow into your brain, and mess with you in the best way possible. It's a pitch-black tale of moral ambiguity, with sympathetic characters facing a home-grown apocalypse of twisted faith, fire, and madness. It's one of the strongest horror debuts in recent memory, which not only entertains but provides penetrating insight into a dark chapter of American history. This is horror done right.

   – Tim Waggoner, Bram Stoker Award-winning author of LIKE DEATH

An absorbing blend of history and narrative fiction which elevates the Waco tragedy into an unforgettable exploration of society, faith, and truth. BREAKING THE WORLD by Jerry Gordon is a compelling novel that thunders, and challenges, from page one. The characters are genuine, the struggles throughout are powerful, balanced, and thoughtful. The novel's conclusion and Gordon's ideas within do what great fiction often hopes to – defies and then transcends what we thought we knew.

   – Geoffrey Girard, Bram Stoker-nominated author of PROJECT CAIN and TRUTHERS

Cover art by Noah Aust.

Jacket design by Mikio Murakami.

ISBN 978-1-937009-64-9 (TPB) 978-1-937009-68-7 (HC)

Apex Publications, LLC
PO Box 24323
Lexington, KY 40524

Also available as a DRM-free eBook.

Visit us at www.apexbookcompany.com.

For Jill and Will

PART ONE

The belief in a supernatural source of evil is not necessary; men alone are quite capable of every wickedness.

Joseph Conrad

OPERATION SHOWTIME

SCRUBBING DRIED PISS OFF THE PORCELAIN GOD OF BINGE drinkers and sloppy athletes gave me a lot of time to think. Not about the small stuff, like getting ratted out by *Skywalker* for pinching three beers after last night's band practice, or how the church's 'true believers' never ended up on their precious knees cleaning gym toilets. No, the early morning smell of bleach and urine led to highly motivated thoughts of escape. Marshal and Rachel were already old enough. In three months, I'd finally have my driver's license, and we could all run away together.

The distant echo of firecrackers interrupted my half-awake thoughts. I hopped up from the toilet, certain Marshal was pulling off some killer prank without me. Dropping the scrub brush on the cheap linoleum floor, I yanked off my yellow rubber gloves and made a run for the bathroom door.

The gymnasium was empty. I looked toward the back exit and then shifted my attention to the double doors that connected the basketball court to the church. Another barrage of fireworks went off in that direction, near the front of the building.

Eager to get in on the action, I bolted for the church doors. Someone shouted at me for running through the chapel, couldn't tell you who. I sprinted up the main aisle, trading the bright pastel glow of 1980s stained glass for an unusually dark entryway. I stumbled over something near the front doors and ended up face first on the shoe mat.

Tiny shafts of light poured in through a bunch of holes in the closed metal doors. Someone screamed and I heard another round of firecrackers, this time halfway up the front stairs. Before I could make any sense out of the holes or Marshal's prank, I felt something bite my ear. I tried to stand up, but David dove on me.

He had a gun in his hand that he fired at the top of the stairway. A lone figure slumped in the shadows, sliding partway down the steps. Despite the gunshot ringing in my ear, I could hear Rachel's dad in the nearby telephone room. "Do ye hear me?" he screamed, his Scottish brogue increasing with volume. "There are women and children here!"

Bursts of gunfire echoed down the dim hallway that led to the cafeteria and men's dorms. Within seconds the whole building rumbled with the sound of low flying helicopters.

"For God's sake!" Rachel's dad continued. "You're shooting at innocent women and children!"

Jimmy joined us in the entryway, firing his rifle down the long hall as fast as he could pull the trigger. A pair of explosions rocked the second floor, sending chunks of ceiling tile down on us.

"Grenades," David said, crouching to reload his handgun. He turned to Jimmy. "How's it look?"

"The hallway's clear. Upstairs through the cafeteria?"

"What's happening?" I asked. "I don't—"

David pulled me up by the scruff of my Rolling Stones T-shirt. "It's not safe out here. Get in the phone room with Liam. You hear me?"

The helicopters made another pass, this time so close to the church that I could feel the vibration of the rotors in my chest. I looked up at him, nodding.

"Good," David said, but he was already turning back to Jimmy. "Let's go!"

Jimmy and David ran down the long hall while I darted into the wood-paneled phone room. Liam had a handgun on the floor next to him, but he didn't try to pick it up. He hugged the ground, motioning me to do the same, the phone pressed to his ear.

"What do ye mean, you cannot reach them? There have to be at least a hundred shooting at us. I've got a fifteen-year-old boy on the floor next to me shot in the head!"

I reached for my ear, shocked to find a thumb-sized chunk missing. Fresh blood soaked my hand, trickling down the side of my arm. It wasn't thick and sticky like in the movies. I looked back to the door and the entryway beyond it. I had to find the rest of my ear so they could sew it back on.

"Yeah, 'oh shit' is right. You've got to get these crazy dobbers to back off before they kill more kids. They've got helicopters. How can they not have radios?"

I stumbled back into the hallway, using my hand as a compress to stop the bleeding. The air was heavy with dust from broken ceiling tiles. The mangled grid that once suspended them shuddered above my head.

"Cyrus, get back here!"

I bent down and started sifting through the debris. It seemed like firecrackers were going off all around me. I could hear them in the gym and the chapel and upstairs, along with the sound of hurried footsteps.

Gunshots, not firecrackers, I reminded myself.

I heard Nick at the other end of the hall screaming for help. I wanted to find the rest of my ear, but the more he screamed, the worse he sounded. The heavy fighting seemed to have moved upstairs, near David's room, so I dashed down the long hall toward his voice.

Just past the kitchen, I slipped and fell. Several inches of water covered the floor on the far end of the men's dorm. I heard breaking glass in the room across from me and decided to crawl the rest of the way. My clothes were soaked in no time. When I got to Nick's room, I froze.

He was lying against the side of his bed in a pool of water and blood. Someone had shot out the water storage tanks just outside his bedroom window. Whatever pain I thought I felt melted away as I rushed to his side. He held his light blue jacket tight to his chest, trying to stop the blood from pouring out.

"Hang in there, Big Boy," I said. David always called him Big Boy. The corner of Nick's mouth trembled with a smile. Skin-and-bones, white-boy Cyrus, not even a man, calling him beefy. "Can I get a look at your chest?"

"I was eating French toast in bed," he replied.

I tried to adopt my mom's clinical tone. "I need to take a look under your jacket, Nick."

He coughed up blood as he nodded. I unzipped his jacket and my heart sank. Blood poured out of him like a fountain only to be washed away by the water coming in from the broken window.

"Tell Bev," he whispered, "I'll wait for her."

I used the corner of his bedspread as a compress, but the bleeding wouldn't stop. I didn't know what to do. Mom was the nurse. I searched the room for a pair of belts, something I could daisy chain into a tourniquet, but the helicopters returned and I had to drop to the floor.

The deep, throaty sound of heavy-caliber machine guns accompanied their strafing run. The room's wooden doorframe splintered, pictures on the dresser shattered, and an urn containing Nick's mom burst, filling the room with a cloud of her remains.

"Tell her I'll wait."

And with that final promise, Nick died.

My mouth opened but I couldn't find words. He passed away looking at my stupid, gobsmacked face. I started to rush back to his side, but another round of gunfire held me back. I just wanted to hold him so he'd know he wasn't alone. He deserved so much more than this.

"Cyrus, is he okay?"

Oliver crawled past the doorway with Marshal in tow. I shook my head, tears streaming down my face. He didn't wait for me to get it together. He kept moving.

"Come on, Cyrus!" Marshal motioned for me to follow him. "It's not safe up here."

"Where's Rachel?" I asked, trying to choke back tears.

"I don't know."

A loud explosion rocked the nearby cafeteria. I crawled after Marshal to a trapdoor at the end of the men's dorm. The metal hatch creaked loudly when Oliver pulled it open. We followed him down the cold metal ladder connecting the church to a dirt cellar and broken down school bus. The men had buried the derelict bus as a makeshift tornado shelter. The trapdoor clanked shut behind us, muffling the sound of gunfire.

Being the only adult, Oliver told us to wait while he grabbed a flashlight out of the school bus. I buried my hands deep in my jean pockets and tried to keep my teeth from chattering in the dark. The winters in Texas seemed mild compared to upstate New York, but my clothes were soaked.

When Oliver came back, he used his gray sweatshirt to muffle the small beam of light. Marshal had a dazed, skittish look about him. His hair, still matted from sleep, curled up like Wolverine on one side. His bathrobe and Aggies Nation T-shirt sported fresh bloodstains. We heard muted explosions upstairs.

"Flashbang grenades," Oliver said in a calm voice. I couldn't help but notice the gun tucked into his faded jeans. "Cyrus, did you get shot?"

"In the ear."

"Dude, that's awesome. Wait until Rachel finds out." Marshal must have seen the look in my eyes because he quickly added, "I'm sure she's fine."

Oliver checked my ear while Marshal and I tried not to contemplate life at Mount Carmel without Rachel. We were the trinity of nonbelievers. The self-imposed outcasts, dragged here by our crazy families. Or, in Marshal's case, running from his.

"Don't worry, Cyrus." Oliver pulled the flashlight away from my ear. "We'll find the rest of it."

The back end of the buried school bus led to a small area the men had excavated for an outside entrance. They'd poured a concrete floor and the first two steps, but a temporary plywood roof still covered the half-finished project.

Oliver decided to risk a peek outside. He handed Marshal the flashlight and proceeded to crawl out through the back of the bus. He didn't get far.

"Come out, or we'll shoot!" a voice screamed from above.

The voice didn't wait for a response before firing a whole magazine into the tunnel. I heard Oliver return fire and then, after a furious exchange of bullets, silence.

"What do we do?" Marshal whispered.

"We stay down. We stay quiet."

I couldn't help but think about all the times David had said 'they' would come for us. The whole congregation repeated his doomsday proclamation like some kind of nutbar mantra, as if the chariots and shields of the ancient prophecies of Nahum could somehow be applied to the modern world. I always thought he used the threat of attack as a boogeyman, something to keep the faithful in line. Now I was too scared to move.

Neither of us expected Oliver to crawl back from the bus, but he did. Marshal used his robe to mute the flashlight. As improbable as the firefight had made it sound, Oliver didn't have a scratch on him. He seemed just as surprised as us, and for a brief moment, our spirits soared with relief.

Then the guns stopped.

AFTERMATH

I DON'T KNOW HOW LONG WE WAITED IN THE DARK OF THE emergency shelter. It felt like three lifetimes. We traded glances in silence, fearing the worst. I pulled my knees close to my chest and rocked myself in the back of that buried school bus, trying to will Rachel to safety. I didn't want to go upstairs and find her and the rest of the church massacred by automatic gunfire.

"What do you think?" Marshal asked Oliver.

"I say we wait." From the sound of his voice, I could tell Oliver's fears mirrored my own. "Maybe they won't realize we're down here."

"I don't know." Marshal turned to me. "Rachel might need our help."

"Or she might already be dead and praying from up above you're smart enough to stay put," Oliver chided.

"Don't say that!" I tried not to raise my voice, but I felt like knocking Oliver's big mouth down his throat. "You don't know what you're talking about."

"And you think you do?" The pain in Oliver's voice reminded me that he had a wife and daughter upstairs. "Just shut up, okay?"

I felt like a self-involved jerk.

9

"Sorry," I whispered. "I'm sure—"

"Well, I'm not, so zip it."

We all jumped at the sound of the shelter's trapdoor creaking open.

"Cease fire! Cease fire!" a familiar voice screamed down the dark hole. "Any folks down there?"

We nearly knocked each other over standing up.

"Who's down there? Speak up!"

"It's Oliver. I've got Marshal and Cyrus with me."

"Well, come on, boys. We've got wounded!"

For an instant, the three of us froze. Stepping out of the bus meant stepping into a future none of us were ready to face. There had been too many bullets and explosions. Not everyone would be as lucky as Oliver.

"People need our help," Oliver said, as if trying to convince himself to move. "Let's get to it."

I nodded, following him out the front of the bus and up the ladder. When I got to the top, my jaw dropped. The long hall looked like someone had rented it out for a *Die Hard* movie. Bullet holes and debris littered the length of the water-soaked dorm. Stepping over broken glass and chunks of soggy ceiling tile, I caught a glimpse of poor Nick, lying on the floor. I could have died right there, next to him.

The thought sent me bolting down the hallway to find Rachel. Marshal chased after me, almost slipping on the wet floor when I made a sharp left at the kitchen. The cafeteria windows were completely blown out. The corner table that had served as our lunchtime refuge from the God Squad, smashed to bits. I stumbled over chunks of concrete and a small crater in the floor, running up the back steps. Halfway up, I ran smack into Rachel.

"Cyrus!" she screamed, hugging me so tight I couldn't speak. I could feel the tears streaming down her face; her chest pressed so close to mine that our heartbeats raced for each other. If I was half a man, I would have kissed her right then, but I didn't. I just held her tight, drinking in the smell of her dark brown hair and the warmth of her trembling body against mine. She still had on last night's tight red flannel shirt. Grunge never felt so good.

Marshal took the stairs at a slower pace, giving me a moment with Rachel before joining our hug. We all started crying and it didn't matter that we looked uncool. When Rachel pulled away from me, she had blood on the left side of her face. I started to panic, but then realized the blood was mine. I could see the look of fear in her eyes as she reached for my ear.

"I'm okay," I reassured her.

"It's only a flesh wound," Marshal added in a half-hearted Monty Python voice. We hugged even harder.

"Have you seen your mum yet?" Rachel asked, stepping back to wipe away her tears. The ever-so-faint Scottish lilt in her voice never failed to make her even more attractive to me.

"Not yet. She okay?" I asked, realizing the question should have occurred to me much sooner.

"She's fine, but they shot David," Rachel said. "She's with him now."

Rachel grabbed my hand and the three of us headed upstairs. The second floor didn't look like a movie set; it looked like Hell on Earth. Bullets littered the main corridor. Doors were knocked in. Sections of the floor and walls had collapsed. I saw Oliver hugging his wife, Karen, and their daughter, Maddie. For a moment, I told myself everything looked worse than it really was. Four dead bodies later, I lost that hope.

Rachel led me past Debbie as quickly as she could. The retired cop's lifeless body dangled off the top of one of the girl's bunk beds. The rifle she had used to defend herself rested on the floor below. Even from behind, you could tell they shot her in the head. The back half of her skull was missing.

Then I saw Mrs. Jankis and her granddaughter clutching each other under a bed. The dark pool of blood surrounding them told the rest of the story. At least they looked peaceful.

The last body amounted to just a severed arm, some unintended victim of a grenade exploding in the confined space of the hallway between David's bedroom and the gun room.

It looked like some kind of crazy video game gone mad. I squeezed Rachel's hand tight as I stepped over the dismembered limb, realizing it belonged to Bev as I passed by her open door. Nick didn't have to wait for her after all.

We found David sprawled out on the catwalk suspended over the gymnasium. Blood soaked his rumpled white dress shirt and blue jeans. From the looks of it, they'd shot him in the chest and wrist. My mom knelt beside him, tending to his wounds. Rachel's dad, Liam, paced behind her.

"He jumped me out of the blue," David said. "That bullet spun me around like a 250-pound man kicking you in the side."

"Get me the other med kit," Mom ordered, "the one in the front office."

Liam raced past us and down the steps near David's bedroom, giving us space to edge closer. I'd never seen David so pale. He seemed just as shocked as the rest of us. "I tried to calm them down," he told my mom, "I swear. They weren't having any of it."

He started to sit up but Mom stopped him.

"You've got to help me keep pressure on the wound." She examined his injured wrist. "Can you move your fingers for me?"

David followed her instructions, but the look on his face said something wasn't right. "I can't feel my thumb," he muttered.

"There isn't a lot of damage," Mom said. "The bullet must have injured a nerve."

Liam came back with the med kit, and I opened it for Mom. As she started patching David up, his attention drifted to me.

"You okay, Cyrus? Your head doesn't look so good."

I'd be lying if I said it didn't bother me that he would ask before my own mom, but I knew she put me second. "I'll be okay. Thanks for saving me."

"When I took your mom as my wife, I'd like to think I gained a son. You may not be my blood, but you are one of my children."

I bit back the urge to argue with him. Rachel's dad, sensing the tension, jumped into the conversation. "What happened?" he asked. "I was eating breakfast when all hell broke loose."

"Well," David paused to lick the blood away from the corner of his lips, "they saddled up in a pair of long cattle trailers, guns all locked and cocked. I went outside to see if we could talk this out. I even told them we had women and children inside. They rushed the building screaming 'police' and 'search warrant,' told me to get down. As soon as I took a step backward, they opened fire. I got the door closed, but they shot clean through it. Hit old man Taylor twice."

"Is that when they shot you?" I asked.

"You let him tell his story," my mom admonished.

"It's okay, Faith. The kids have as much a right to know as any of us. Maybe more, seeing how they're so young and we just put their lives at risk."

I didn't like being called a kid, none of us did, but I always appreciated the way David stuck up for me. When he took my mom as one of his 'spiritual wives,' there was a big uproar in the church about the fact that I refused to call him Dad. Upset everyone but him. He told me he grew up without a father and understood, promised he'd look out for me just the same.

"A couple of our boys must have thought the Feds hit me, because they started returning fire and it all went south in a hurry. I managed to make it upstairs and get the women and children under their beds. But with those helicopters shooting down at us, I didn't think anyone was safe."

David grimaced as Mom blotted disinfectant on his chest wound. She said he should count his blessings. The bullet appeared to have passed clean through. If she could get the bleeding stopped and stave off infection, he'd have a good chance at a full recovery. The news seemed to add a touch of color to his otherwise clammy cheeks.

"Why'd they stop?" Marshal asked. "We were down in the shelter and they just stopped."

"Ran out of ammo," David replied. "They didn't have any

interest in a ceasefire until they'd emptied every gun they had into our church. Liam told them they could have one if they promised to leave our property and never come back."

Rodney came running down the catwalk with a cordless phone in his hand. David took the phone and tried to reposition his back against the metal railing. "This is David Koresh."

He listened to the man on the phone for a minute and then started shaking his head. "No. No. No. Let me tell you something. You brought a bunch of guys out here and you killed some of my children. We told you we wanted to talk, but you wanted to shoot first. Now there's a bunch of us dead and there's a bunch of you guys dead. That's your fault."

I wished I could hear the whole conversation. We all did. The group hovering behind us continued to grow.

"Demands?" David's voice raised a full octave. "Are you kidding me? Listen, you're not from around these parts, so let me explain something to you. The people that live out here have come from all around the world to hear my teachings on the Bible. They aren't hostages. They can come and go as they please. At least, they could before you started shooting up the place. Now they're all scared you're going to kill them."

I still couldn't wrap my brain around the idea that the government had just attacked a church. I didn't believe in David's Seven Seals crap, but we lived in America, not the Soviet Union. We had a constitution and laws to protect people's right to worship whatever idiotic god they wanted.

"Listen," David's voice faltered, "I'm lying here on the floor with two bullet holes in me. I doubt I could stand right now if I tried. How in the world could I be keeping over a hundred people hostage?"

PART TWO

Wild, dark times are rumbling toward us, and the prophet who wishes to write a new apocalypse will have to invent entirely new beasts.

Heinrich Heine

CEASEFIRE

WHILE THE ATF EVACUATED THEIR DEAD AND WOUNDED, WE tended to our own. Mom couldn't save old man Taylor. He bled out near the front door, scared to his last breath. Watching him die, I realized that I'd tripped over his body in my race to the front door.

I told him I was sorry, but I don't think he understood me. After he passed, Mom tried to patch up my ear, but I insisted she tend to the wounded women and children first. We never found the missing chunk.

The tenuous ceasefire, when paired with the realities of decomposition, demanded quick action. I volunteered to help the men bury our dead under the dirt floor of the tornado shelter. We split up, two to a hole, and dug in fifteen-minute shifts. Well, most of us did.

Marshal had a body as big as his heart, which is a roundabout way of saying he wasn't built for digging. I let him handle the easy work, the first couple feet. When he started breathing heavy, I took over.

More than just a sore spot, Marshal's size constantly reminded him that he had failed to live up to his family's standards. Sure, he could fish and hunt and survive in the woods without help. His dad made sure of that. But he was also fat and bookish and geeky in a way his father could never understand or accept. His pasty-white exterior, inherited from his mother, didn't help. There was a path and a way set forth by his Sioux ancestors, and Marshal didn't have the slightest idea how to find it.

The two of us didn't talk while digging Nick's hole. No one did. We were all shell-shocked by the echo of bullets, the guilt of surviving, the strangeness of bodies wrapped in plain white sheets without coffins or pallbearers or flowers. I'd only been to one funeral. I can't say the tradition and ceremony of it helped much, but it definitely did more for me than digging graves in a cold dirt cellar.

I wondered what my older brother would have thought about all this as I continued to dig. I know it sounds ridiculous. I don't even believe in God, much less an afterlife with pearly gates and loved ones looking down at you from up high. I just wonder sometimes what he would be like if he'd lived. Would Mom and Dad still be together? Would we be close like Marshal and me?

When we finished digging, Oliver said a few kind words over each of the six graves and I silently apologized to Nick and old man Taylor for not saving them. I never felt particularly close to Taylor. He was drawn to Mount Carmel by a deep need for spirituality I didn't share or understand, but he was decent to me. And he left behind a family that would never be able to fill the void left by his loss.

I tried not to think about Nick and Bev. It was hard enough to convince the adults that Marshal and I were old enough to help. I wasn't about to prove we weren't up to the task by breaking down over Nick's grave. But if I lived to be a hundred, I'd never forget the look on his face as he passed.

I wanted to burn my clothes when we finished filling in the graves, but I knew Mom would never stand for the waste. She would find a way to get the blood and dirt out. With the water storage tanks all shot up, Marshal and I trucked small buckets of water to the men's communal bathroom.

Looking in the mirror, I tugged at my short brown hair. Zero chance it would hide the bandaged ear. Maybe it would give me some badly needed street cred. I sneered at myself and then gave up on the idea. Punk died years ago, and I didn't have a hard enough face. I looked like the boy next door with the tip of his ear shot off.

Going back to the room I shared with Marshal, I pulled a fresh pair of jeans and a gray hooded sweatshirt off the pile of clean laundry at the bottom of my side of the closet. After a quick glance in the mirror on the back of our door, I pulled the hood over my ear. Marshal told me I should wear my bandages loud and proud. I told him to stuff it.

By the time we got back to the chapel, someone had wheeled the big forty-inch projection TV onto the stage. The majority of the congregation huddled around it. David sat on the ground, propped up against a choir chair. He looked worse than when I left him. Sweat beaded on his forehead and his eyes seemed strained and unfocused. No one spoke. It didn't take long to figure out why.

The nightly news showed a long convoy of FBI vehicles heading down the dusty gravel roads we all knew led to Mount Carmel. Rachel spotted me and motioned for the two of us to join her behind the stage.

"Can you believe it?" she asked, taking a seat on the steps that led up to the gym catwalk where we found David had been shot. "They're fixing to bring in tanks and everything. It's mad."

I looked back at the television, but I couldn't make out what the news anchor was saying over the helicopter footage. I just knew it couldn't be good.

"They keep calling the church a cult and saying that David thinks he's Jesus come to end the world."

"That's crazy," Marshal said. "Why are they doing this?"

"Your ATF says we've been stockpiling weapons and training an army to bring about the End of Days." Rachel rubbed her eyes. She looked like she'd been crying. "We don't have that many guns, do we, Marshal?"

"My jackass dad has more than we do, and most of what we've got is for selling at the gun shows. It's all legal. David's got a business partner with the permits and everything. Why would they make something like that up?"

Marshal looked to me for an answer.

"No idea, but we've got to get out of here before somebody rings the bell for round two. I know we were planning on getting our own apartment later this year, after I got my license, but I can't think of a better reason to move things up." I hesitated before looking at Rachel. "You still want to live with us, right?"

"Of course." She bopped me on the forehead. "You're my boys. The only thing worse than living here is, well, you know, dying here. Maybe we could go out waving white T-shirts or something, let your government know we give up."

"That won't work," Marshal said. "They'll put us in foster care, for sure. No way they let us stay together. We're going to have to sneak out."

A long silence followed. Marshal knew a whole lot more about foster homes than we did. The government pulled him off the reservation when his dad went to prison. He'd bounced between group homes, distant aunts, and his mom, all before moving to Texas. It would be an understatement to say the few stories he'd told me weren't good.

"Fair play," Rachel said. "We can't let them split us up, and we can't stay here."

I started to ask Marshal if he had any ideas on how we were going to sneak past an FBI siege, but a chorus of gasps interrupted the thought. We returned to the group and found Craig Sullivan, the local bar owner that hosted our band's gigs, on television. He claimed David had a military-grade bunker under the church and funded his arsenal of guns by selling drugs to high school kids.

"What the heck is he talking about?" Because I was underage, I could only be in the bar when the band performed, but I had spent months around Craig. He used to come out to the church and jam with us on his off nights. He knew there were no drugs out here, much less dealers. And the idea that we had a bunker under the church. I couldn't understand why he would lie about something so stupid, so easily proved wrong.

An interview with an ATF agent followed. He used the word ambush to describe our vicious attack of law enforcement officers. We all stood there with our mouths wide open. Did the news media not understand the government had attacked us? As a nonbeliever, I couldn't fathom the outright lies being passed off as evidence that we were a danger to the citizens of Texas. Were they painting us all evil to justify their own actions? I mean, no way America would stand for the government pointing tanks at a church, right?

As deception piled on deception, the FBI convoy drew closer to Mount Carmel. The news anchor moved on to a story about a meningitis outbreak in Mexico, but the world's judgment weighed on us all.

"We've got to get out of here," Marshal repeated.

Sensing the congregation's need for guidance and David's inability to provide it in his current condition, Liam set up a watch schedule and suggested we move bunk beds into the cement vault to protect the women and children from stray bullets. I half-listened, nodding when tasked with moving beds.

Mainly, I watched Mom checking David's bandages as he watched the news. The outbreak in Mexico had killed nineteen and sent almost five hundred to the hospital. After burying six members of the church, including one that had died right next to me, the immensity of those numbers carried more meaning.

"Do you see it, Cyrus?" David asked.

I could feel my ears turn red and throb as everyone around me went silent.

"You do." He looked my way. "I know you do."

David struggled to stand, using the choir chair and my mom for balance. "Zechariah and Ezekiel saw this day coming," he said in his quiet, understated way. "Babylon may forsake us, brand us evil for our devout pursuit of Scripture, but don't you worry none.

God will make them pay for rejecting us, for rejecting His message."

Letting go of Mom, he stood, in calm defiance of his injuries.

"Go now," he said. "Liam has given you all important works. Trust God to take care of the rest."

The weight of outside judgment seemed to lift with David's words, and the faithful stood with a renewed sense of purpose. I'd read the Bible and studied the Seals, if for no other reason than to get Mom off my back. Still, I had no idea what David's bullet-addled mind had in store for us.

"Come on," Marshal said. "They've paired us up with Skywalker."

"I'm still pissed about him ratting me out last night. You can move beds with him. I'll take Rachel."

"Shocker." Marshal rolled his eyes at me to emphasize just how much he didn't buy my excuse.

"Hey, you weren't stuck scrubbing toilets at o-six-crazy because of him. And you could've been," I said, reminding him that I'd taken the fall for both of us.

Marshal raised his hands in mock defeat.

I can't remember what Seventh Day Adventist rock Skywalker crawled out from under. He came to Mount Carmel with his Uncle Rick. The only thing that separated him from the average prophecy junky: the worn, thrift-store *Star Wars* T-shirt he arrived in. Marshal assumed he'd found us a kindred spirit and started talking to him about Wookies and Death Stars and the possibility of two more trilogies. Turned out the kid had never seen a movie, much less the greatest one of all time. He thought we were crazy.

Putting Marshal and Skywalker together made practical sense. The Bible nerd was no stranger to hard work and could shoulder more than his half of the load. I'd like to think I could do the same for Rachel, but she'd probably argue the reverse.

Dragging frames and mattresses from the girls' upstairs dorm to the vault gave us time together, but the work didn't lend itself to heartfelt conversation. And to be honest, it doesn't take much of anything to get me to chicken out when it comes to talking about my feelings. I'm not exactly my dad when it comes to the ladies.

I lost count of the number of trips we made up and down the back steps. Once, bending a mattress around a tight corner, we were smushed together and there was a moment, an almost kiss. The work went much easier after that.

We managed to cram fifteen bunks into the vault. Thirty beds total. With all but the pregnant women doubling up, we had just enough room. The men piled mattresses on the floor near watch points around the church. That might sound crazy, but the government was literally surrounding us with tanks. Everyone feared for their lives.

Marshal and I wanted to go with the men, but we weren't allowed. Only a handful of church members had experience with guns, and they didn't have the luxury of babysitting us. We were too young to fight and too old to hide.

I'd never fired a gun, but Marshal had taught me and Rachel how to use a crossbow last summer. Before sundown, we managed to snag all three bows out of storage. We posted watch over the vault. Oliver pulled his mattress into the nearby kitchen and seemed happy to let us pretend to protect the women and children.

Late that night, with Rachel asleep behind us, Marshal broke the long silence with a warning. "You know she's going to run off with the first biker that comes along."

"What are you talking about?"

"Rachel. Look, you know I love you like a brother. And you've got this whole Jagger meets Holden Caulfield thing going for you, singing in David's band and all. But compared to the outside world, you're pretty tame."

"So?"

"So Rachel's the type of girl who gets bored easy. Once she sees what's out there in the big wide world, you don't stand a chance."

"She's deeper than that," I said with a certainty half meant to convince myself. I had enough to worry about with David taking wives younger than her. I didn't need to add the rest of the world. Besides, Marshal hadn't seen the look in her eyes this afternoon when we got smushed together or felt the beat of her heart as she wrapped her arms around me after the attack.

I looked back at her. She even snored sexy. Soft, shallow noises that drew you closer. Her tiny nose ring glinted in the vault's pale nightlight. She got that piercing in India, after her mother died. I bet Marshal didn't know that.

"And who the hell is Holden Caulfield?"

SIGNS AND PORTENTS

"Cyrus, wake up. Come on, dude. We've got to get to the chapel. Stat."

"What?" I turned over, trading the warmth of my pillow for the cold concrete of the vault's entrance. The moment my bandaged ear hit the hard floor, pain shattered the last remnants of sleep.

I sat up, cupping my ear. My clenched teeth muffled the stream of curse words that followed. I rubbed my eyes and tried to focus on my surroundings. Dawn cast a warm glow through the shattered cafeteria windows.

"What's going on?" I asked.

"They shot Jimmy. We're all meeting in the chapel."

The words didn't want to register.

"Jimmy? Where?"

"I don't know any more than you do. Come on, princess."

Marshal offered me his hand. I took it and pulled myself up. Despite the thick sleeping bag, my body had never felt stiffer. I rubbed my neck, careful to avoid my ear and the vision-blurring pain that exploded from it every time it was bumped. From the look of the bags under Marshal's eyes, he had let me sleep most of the night.

"Where's Rachel?" I asked.

"She got up early and went to see if her dad knew anything."

I stumbled after Marshal. The adults had cleared the kitchen and long hall of glass and sharp debris, but soggy chunks of drywall and ceiling tile still floated in orphaned pools of water, giving the church the look of an abandoned construction site. I wanted to brush my teeth, or at least change my underwear.

Stepping into the chapel, I blended into the disheveled congregation. The television was on, but someone had muted the sound. The room knelt in silent prayer. I didn't see Rachel or her father. David and my mom were also absent.

Marshal and I walked down the center aisle, invisible to the self-proclaimed Stars of David. We climbed onto the stage, looking for the remote so we could at least turn on the closed captioning. Let the congregation pray. We needed real answers.

Before either of us could find the remote, Liam came down the stairs from David's room with Rachel following close behind. Like us, she still wore yesterday's clothes. She just looked better in them.

"I'm afraid I have some very bad news for you," Liam said to the congregation, walking to the foot of the stage. "The FBI shot our poor Jimmy just before dawn. I sent the lad out to the water tanks to see if he could get the pumps running again. Whatever's wrong with them, he ended up climbing the tower. They mistook him for a sniper."

"Was he armed?" Oliver's wife asked.

"He had on a tool belt," Liam replied. "No guns."

That crushed any hope the FBI would be reasonable where the ATF had been rash and aggressive. Clearly, they were just as trigger happy. We could only hope they had better negotiators.

"David isn't well enough to come down, but he wanted me to pass along a reminder that he will think no less of any member of this church if you want or need to leave. There's no shame in following your heart. Most of you have family out there worried sick.

"Personally, and this is just me speaking here, I'd ask you to come forward before going out there, so we can contact the FBI in advance and avoid another senseless tragedy."

Marshal and I traded glances. Sneaking out had just become a much more dangerous option. While Liam answered questions, Rachel motioned us over to the back stairs.

"David needs to see you," she whispered.

I had a hard time imagining what he wanted with us. Her voice had an odd tone to it. Something seemed off about her this morning. The way she came down the steps like a dutiful daughter. Marshal and I started up the steps, but she stopped him.

"Just Cyrus."

Marshal smiled like he had just gotten out of a trip to the principal's office. He didn't appear concerned at all. Maybe my imagination was getting the best of me.

"You're not in trouble," Rachel added with a goofy smirk that didn't ease the weird sense of dread settling into the pit of my stomach.

I walked upstairs and into David's room. Someone had cleared it of furniture, save a mattress on the floor and a dresser with a small TV on top. He sat on the floor against the dingy, powder-burned wall, Mom and another wife at his side. Three men paced the edges of the room, all armed.

The shattered windows had been boarded up, and a speaker phone sat on the floor next to David. He took a swig of orange juice from a nearly empty gallon jug and continued his thought.

"I keep telling you boys, this is our home. Nobody's being held hostage."

"Okay, David." The voice on the other side of the phone sounded calm, almost parental. "It's your house. We understand that. Just let a few of the kids go so we can see you're treating them okay. Do that and we'll get you some medical attention."

"Now, Liam already went through that with your boys. We don't want anything to do with your medicine after what you did here. And as far as letting people go, it's not up to me whether they stay or leave."

"Then who is it up to, David? God?"

"Big picture? Sure, we're talking God." David pulled up the bottom of his white tank top and used it to wipe the corner of his nose. "But you know that's not what I mean."

"We don't know what you mean, David. We need you to be clear."

"I have been nothing but straight with your boys, which is more than I can say for you. After you ran out of ammo, shooting up our women and children, we let you go on the promise that you would leave our home and never come back."

"You know we can't do that."

"Then you shouldn't have promised it."

"I don't disagree," the man on the phone said, "but I can't do anything about that now. People have been killed—on both sides of this. ATF is going to have to answer for that, same as you. But before that can happen, we've got to get those children out of harm's way."

"You boys are the only harm's way they're in." David took another swig of juice. "My congregation is free to go any time they choose. I'm bleeding to death on the floor here, man. I'm not holding anyone back."

"Do they know they can leave?"

"You have got to be kidding me." David took the last swig of orange juice and motioned for me to come get his empty. "You can tell you're on speaker phone, right? There are half a dozen people with me right now, including a boy your men shot in the head. Say hello, Cyrus."

I froze, empty jug in hand.

"Um ... hello."

"Are you okay, son? This is Agent Randal Shepherd. You can call me Shep. Do you need medical attention?"

I looked to David and my mom. They both nodded I should continue. The look in Mom's eyes said whether I wanted to or not.

"My mom's a nurse. I'm okay."

"Do you realize you can leave here? We're not here to hurt you. We're here to help."

"Seriously?" I almost couldn't wrap my brain around the insanity of his words. "You sure have a sick way of showing it."

"I don't know what you've been told, but—"

"My friend Nick died right in front of me. He was eating breakfast in bed when you shot him. Mrs. Jankis and Peggy—they were hiding under their bed, terrified, when you killed them. None of them had guns. They didn't even know how to shoot a gun. Now you want to tell me that you're here to help? Do you have any idea how crazy that sounds? How sick?"

My bandaged ear started throbbing. My face reddened with anger and fear that I had just said something that could provoke another attack.

"You boys ain't winning many friends in our house," David said. "Liam and I've been talking. I think we're going to need a third party in here."

Another long silence followed. I looked to my mom, afraid of the punishment soon to follow my outburst, but the look on her face almost seemed proud. I took a deep breath and hoped she was right and I didn't just screw everything up.

"What do you mean, a third party?"

"Well," David said, "here's the thing. It's clear you don't trust me. I don't think there's anything I can say to change that. And if you're honest with yourself, you've got to admit that you've given my family and my church every reason in the world not to trust you. We need someone neutral to talk us through this here impasse. Someone we can both learn to trust."

"I don't think my bosses are going to go for that, David. They're not going to let this thing drag on for weeks. Not with the news media camped out all around us."

"I'm watching tanks roll in on CNN while you're trying to tell me you want to resolve this all peaceful-like. What kind of country do we live in that would use tanks on its own citizens?"

"You've got to believe me. I don't know anything about any tanks. This is the first I'm hearing of it."

"I swear." David ran a hand through his hair. "I might as well be talking to the pizza delivery guy. Why don't you boys figure out what's going on out there and then get back to me."

David leaned forward and hung up the phone, wincing as he fell back against the wall. He took a shallow breath and then looked up at me. "You okay, Cyrus? I didn't mean to put you on the spot like that."

"Yes, you did."

Mom stood, ready to unleash a tirade on me for calling her precious husband and prophet a liar. Before she could get the first word out of her mouth, David stopped her with a small gesture of his hand. He might as well have her on a leash.

"Why don't you give me a moment alone with Cyrus," he said. "I didn't call him up here to embarrass him on the phone."

The men shuffled out of the bedroom with respectful nods. Mom wouldn't go that easy. She squinted her eyes into tiny balls of anger ready to incinerate me for embarrassing her.

"I mean it, Faith. I need to talk to the boy alone."

David's third wife helped Mom find the door. Just before it closed, she looked back long enough to make sure I knew we would be discussing this later.

"I didn't plan on bringing you into the negotiations, Cyrus. I promise you that."

The look on his face reminded me of my father. Far from angry or offended, he seemed disappointed in me. Did he know we were planning to escape? Did someone see the way I held Rachel after the attack? A dozen previously undiscovered rule violations could be the cause of that look.

"Then what do you want?" I asked.

"It's not what I want. It's what I need. With the FBI setting up sniper nests around our church and shooting up anyone that goes outside, I need someone to help keep the other teens safe."

"And you want my help?" I couldn't hide the surprise in my voice.

"Temper aside, you've always been more mature than the others." David took off his thick, aviator-style prescription glasses and rubbed his bloodshot eyes. "I'm not worried about the little ones. They're too scared to run, but the teenagers. I expect some of them are making escape plans stupid enough to get themselves shot or worse. They'll be too embarrassed to come to us before they run. The Feds won't know they're coming."

"What makes you think they'll listen to me?"

"You and your friends may not be true believers, but you are worldly. They'll trust you when it comes to life on the outside. They need to understand what it means to have the government put you in a foster home or jail or worse."

"How do you know we're not planning to leave?" The words tumbled out of my mouth before I could hope to stop them.

"Because you're smarter than that. You saw the news this morning. You know what's coming. There are no atheists in a foxhole."

I looked over at the twelve-inch television on the corner of David's dresser. Someone had turned the sound all the way down, but the news story didn't need it. A reporter stood at an emergency room entrance to a hospital. Below him, the headline read "U.S. Border Closed" in bold letters.

I crossed the room and turned up the volume. The government had confirmed five cases of a new strain of meningitis, two in Austin and three in San Antonio. The head of the CDC said the border closing amounted to a precautionary measure. Given our superior medical facilities and the young age of the patients, they had an excellent chance of survival.

The official cautioned border residents not to panic. The United States would not see an outbreak similar to Mexico, where the death toll had skyrocketed to almost a thousand overnight. I knew what David would say before he even opened his mouth.

"The Second Seal is breaking, Cyrus. Soon Mount Carmel will

be the only place that's safe. I had hoped for more time, for a chance to convince the world, but His wrath is at hand. All I can do now is protect the people here."

"Until the Fourth Seal."

"Everyone dies, Cyrus. I can't undo God's will."

"That's all fine and good for you, but I'm fifteen. I'd like another seventy or eighty years, if you don't mind."

"You think I don't want more? Thirty-three might seem like a lifetime away, but it's not. People came here because they understood the end was near. They know what's coming."

"And what about the rest of us? The ones like Rachel and Marshal and me who don't believe? The ones who got dragged here by their crazy parents?"

"For you, the end is just the beginning. The Fourth Seal only applies to the true believers." David put his glasses back on. "I wish I could give you the life you want. You're a hell of a guitar player and a bright boy, but the world is breaking. These aren't my plans."

"Don't." I rubbed my forehead as if the simple action would help me assemble my thoughts into an argument he could accept. "These people have travelled the world to be with you. They'll stand by you no matter what. You don't need to invent an apocalypse just to hold them together. You're better than that."

"This isn't about me, Cyrus. It never has been. I know you don't like being here at Mount Carmel. You feel like an outcast, like you don't fit in. Don't you think I understand? I was a stuttering, dyslexic kid with visions from God, not the star of the football team. I didn't ask for this life, didn't want it. You may not be a willing student, but you understand Scripture better than just about any kid here. Look at that television and tell me that you don't see Revelation."

I didn't know what to say. He looked like he hadn't slept since they shot him, and I could only claim a few hours on a concrete floor. I didn't even know what meningitis was. The government stooge on TV didn't seem worried. Why should I be?

"Not everything's a sign from God," I finally muttered. "If this was a big deal, they'd be doing a lot more than just hospitalizing people."

"You watched the government kill innocent people here and then lie about it. What makes you so sure they ain't lying about this as well?"

He had a point. I just didn't want to admit it.

"Even if they are lying, it doesn't mean it's the end of the world." I cut him off before he could continue. "I don't think there's anything you could say that would make me believe in the Second Seal. You need to reason with the FBI. You need to find a way out of this standoff before more innocent people die."

"I'm not asking you to believe, Cyrus. I'm asking you to help me keep the other teens from doing something stupid. I don't want more people hurt." I turned away from the television, knowing it would be almost impossible to sneak away if he sold everyone in the church on this being the apocalypse. I had to get Rachel and Marshal out of here before that happened.

"I'll do what I can, but there are no guarantees any of them will listen."

PART THREE

The safest road to Hell is the gradual one—
the gentle slope, soft underfoot,
without sudden turnings,
without milestones,
without signposts.

C.S. Lewis

BEST LAID PLANS

I found Marshal and Skywalker upstairs taking closet doors off their hinges. The men were using the solid wood doors to seal off broken windows and cover the numerous holes in the floor. I'd seen two more groups scavenging wood downstairs. Before long, they'd have the whole place sealed up like a tomb.

Skywalker leaned into a paint-encrusted hinge screw, grunting as he attempted to turn it. He had just about stripped the thing clean when I offered to take a crack. He handed over the Phillips screwdriver without a fight. I told him to grab a quick snack downstairs. He wasn't halfway down the hall before Marshal started peppering me with questions.

"What's going on? He had you up there forever. Are we in trouble?"

"More than you know," I replied, trying to get the screwdriver to catch. Skywalker had done a number on the screw. After a second try, I decided to switch to a different hinge.

"Then what's going on? Rachel wouldn't tell me anything. And she hasn't left her dad's side all morning."

"There's some kind of flu epidemic or something, down in

Mexico. They've closed the border. David thinks it's a plague that will sweep the Earth of nonbelievers."

"The Second Seal," Marshal said, his voice dropping as low as he could manage. "I always knew this day would come."

"Stop messing with me. The last thing I need is for those wingnuts to get to you."

"No worries, I'm impervious to bullshit. It's one of my many secret powers."

I snorted, tossing two screws his way. It didn't take long for curiosity to get the best of him.

"How many people are infected?"

"On our side of the border? Like four or five. But it won't take long for David to turn them into a reason to keep us all here. For our protection and eternal souls and stuff."

"You think he would really do that?"

"It's basically done. He's put me in charge of stopping the other teens from running. Things are about to get seriously apocalyptic in this church. We've got to get out of here before David convinces everyone that it's their responsibility to make us stay."

Oliver and Rodney walked past with a closet door in hand. Marshal knelt beside me, bringing his voice to a whisper. "We can't run. It's too dangerous. I don't want to get accidentally-on-purpose snipered."

"Could we sneak out at night?" I asked.

"Infrared scopes. They'd see us coming from a mile away. And we can't use the phone to warn them without going through Rachel's dad or David. The elders are camped out on the phones twenty-four-seven."

"So we can't run and we can't call. What if we made a banner or something, hung it out one of the second story windows?"

Marshal closed the closet door enough to give me a good view of the bedroom window. A hardwood door had been nailed over it like a coffin lid. I shuddered.

"Even if we get out," Marshal said, "that's just the beginning of our problems. If we're lucky, they'll just split us up and throw us in foster care."

"And if we're not lucky?"

"Juvie or prison."

"Come on, Marshal. They're not going to throw us in prison."

"They could blame us for the dead agents."

"I don't even know how to shoot a gun."

"Yeah, well, I do. And if they bring my crazy dad in for questioning, and he goes all native on them, telling them they don't own the country or threatening a revolution, I'm sunk."

"You think it's going to end better in here? David's not going to give in, not with God's plague striking down his enemies. You think the FBI's just going to get bored and go home?"

"He really thinks the end of the world's going to happen?" Marshal asked. "Now, I mean?"

"It's worse than that. He's counting on it."

Mount Carmel was the only real home Marshal had ever known, and I could see by the look on his face that he was a little scared to leave it. Sure, we all ragged on the place, but it was still home. Even I had to admit I liked singing and playing guitar in David's band.

"We'd have to sell them out," he finally offered. "Lie about things here. We'd be the victims. They'd put us in foster care for sure if we did that. Then we could run away, meet some place safe after the dust settled."

I felt guilty just listening to the idea. It sounded like something my father would do. I wanted to get away, but not like that.

"We'd have to interrupt one of their phone calls and say we want to leave. The way David keeps telling them he's not holding hostages, he'd have to let us go."

"And what happens here?" I asked. "Once we sell the world on them being monsters?"

Marshal took a long time to answer. He had to know how uncomfortable I'd be with the suggestion.

"I don't know," he finally offered.

"Don't know what?" Skywalker asked. He stood in the doorway with a half-empty bottle of Orange Crush. From the goofy look on his face, I could tell he hadn't heard anything important.

"How we're going to get this door off without an axe," Marshal replied.

Skywalker gave both of us a toothy grin and revealed a small hatchet. "Grabbed it from the guys downstairs. I thought it might speed things up."

"Cool," I said. "You want the first swing?"

Skywalker spent the next five minutes chopping at the bottom hinge. The wood finally split and he moved on to the middle of the door with a vengeance that warned me never to piss him off. Pure anger poured out of every swing.

"Oi, Spaceman! Give it a rest!" Rachel leaned against the still attached bedroom door. With her rumpled flannel shirt and worn jean jacket, she looked cool enough to front her own band.

"We've got twenty more of these to take off today," Skywalker said. "We don't have time for more breaks."

"Yeah, yeah. Now bugger off! I need to talk to my boys."

He looked back at us long enough to confirm he wasn't welcome and then buried the small hatchet in the door. "Fine, I'll take another break, but I'm not answering for it if we don't get done."

Rachel rolled her eyes as he huffed out the door. "Touchy, that one. If I didn't know better, I'd swear he was a wee fannyboy. He's practically—"

"Where have you been all day?" Marshal interrupted.

"And what's up with you and your dad?" I asked. "You've been glued to him all morning."

She leaned out into the hallway, peeking down both ends.

"Can't talk about it here. I've got to get back before they miss me."

"Before who misses—"

"Meet me in the back of the bus tonight, after everyone's gone to bed. Midnight."

"How are we supposed to get past the night watch?" Marshal asked. "Somebody will be guarding the shelter hatch."

"There's no 'we' this time. Just Cyrus."

"What about me?"

Rachel's eyes widened as her face mocked Marshal's whiney tone. "What about you?" She looked my way, the expression on her face turning serious. "Midnight. Don't stand me up."

Before either of us could ask another question, she buried her hands deep in her jean jacket pockets and shuffled back into the hall. Oliver and Rodney passed her on their way back to grab another door. Neither of us knew what she was planning, but given all the secrecy, it had to be big.

And I'd have to wait until midnight to find out.

MY CHOICE

THE THREE OF US RIPPED OUT THE REST OF THE UPSTAIRS CLOSET doors that day, breaking for the occasional survey of girls' underwear. Skywalker started it when he snooped a stash of lace bras and thongs hidden in the back of a closet. The black and red underwear belonged to a pair of new members, twins from Australia, here with their mom for a little over a month.

If you had asked me to describe the pair before this discovery, I'm not sure I could have. They faded into the background, which is a hard thing for twins to do. They always wore long skirts and thick turtleneck sweaters. Bland colors and oversized glasses framed by dull brown hair, that's what I pictured when I thought about them. Who could have imagined they were hiding this underneath? My mom's whole "don't judge a book by its cover" thing mattered a whole lot more when applied to girls and underwear.

Mount Carmel didn't have a dress code, but I couldn't imagine underwear this sexy as anything but a protest against being brought here. Maybe they were just like the three of us, nonbelievers dragged to the armpit of Texas and trapped between David and an FBI gone mad. The thought took the fun out of finding their secret stash. It brought me back to Marshal's plan of escape.

With Skywalker tagging along, we didn't get any time to talk about it. To tell you the truth, the thought of selling out everyone in the church shamed me to my core. It felt like a coward's way out, but I couldn't think of a better plan to keep us safe. Tonight, Marshal would expect me to convince Rachel to go along with it.

Would she go with me? With us? The question scared me. She could say no. She could crush my dreams with a single word. I couldn't be madder at myself for letting it come to this. I should have told her how I felt a long time ago. I should never have hidden behind the idea of one day becoming roommates.

Dinner came and went. I still didn't know what to do. The broken water pump that Jimmy died trying to fix led to water rationing. Marshal and I managed enough to brush our teeth and wash our faces, but a shower was out of the question. Eventually, we made it upstairs to change clothes and put on some deodorant. I grabbed my other hooded sweatshirt off the closet floor and put it on, carefully pulling it over my sorry excuse for an ear.

I couldn't tell if Marshal was pissed about being left out of tonight's mystery or just tired of hearing me obsess over Rachel. He seemed more disagreeable with each passing hour. Lack of sleep probably had a lot to do with it. At least David didn't announce the breaking of the Second Seal. We both agreed that made it easier to escape.

We didn't see Rachel that night, when the women and children piled into the vault. I gave the twins from Australia a goofy grin but they either didn't notice or ignored me. As everyone settled in, I noticed that Rodney had camped out in the kitchen and Oliver now watched over the entrance to the buried bus. A little after midnight, Marshal caught Rodney dozing off and motioned me past him.

Oliver jumped a bit when he heard me coming his way but said nothing. He looked down the dim hallway, satisfied himself that we were alone, and waved me past. I opened the trapdoor as slowly as possible, worried the hinge might squeak, but it had been oiled by someone and didn't break the eerie calm.

Oliver closed the hatch behind me, leaving me to feel my way down the ladder and past the dirt graves. Don't ask me why I didn't think to grab a flashlight. Rachel proved smarter. A small hint of light came from the bus.

Rachel waited for me in the back with a green army blanket around her. As I climbed into the seat next to her, I could see faint wisps of my breath in the cold winter air. My teeth chattered.

"I started to worry something had happened to you." She offered up half of her blanket. "Get over here before you catch your death."

Scooting next to Rachel's warm body, I pulled the blanket over me. Alone with her, this close, my mind wanted to turn this into a different midnight, one where half the FBI didn't have us surrounded, one where I could say what I felt.

"I know you want to get out of here." Rachel edged closer, her warm hand reaching for mine. "And I'm sure you and Marshal already have a brilliant plan to make that happen, but I need you to stay with me."

"Stay?" It took a few seconds for the words to register. I tensed up, bracing myself for the possibility that Rachel's dad laid the same apocalyptic garbage on her and she bought it. "We can't stay."

"David's gone pure mental," she said, "and not his normal Scripture-nut sort. He's lost a lot of blood from his gunshot wounds. He's delusional, prattling on about the Second Seal, completely unwilling to negotiate with the FBI. If we don't stop him, a lot of people are going to die."

"You can't stop him, Rachel. That's why we need to get out of here. Now. This isn't a game. The FBI's parking tanks outside. This is going to end bad, very soon."

"Which is why I need you here with me." She edged closer, as if proximity could override my common sense.

"What's going on with you?" I asked. "You haven't left your dad's side all day, and now you've got Oliver waving me past for some kind of secret meeting with a girl after midnight, no questions asked."

"Since when did the rules matter to you?"

"Since never. It's just—"

"You know my dad's a true believer, right?"

"Yeah ..."

"Well, even he knows something's wrong with David. And he's not alone. Oliver. Maurice. Jason. Geoff. There are more of us than you know. Dad says David's got his prophecies all mixed up and out of order. The apocalypse is supposed to be a few years off. We have to stop him before he gets everyone killed."

"We?" I started pulling away but she held tight to my hand. "You can't reason with crazy. David will never listen to your dad or anyone else."

"He listened to you, Cyrus."

"What?"

"My dad spent half the morning trying to convince David not to announce the breaking of the Second Seal. He wouldn't budge. You talked to him for five minutes and changed his mind."

The idea that I had somehow talked David out of something, especially something related to his precious Seals, dumfounded me. It didn't seem possible.

"Whatever you said, it worked. Dad needs your help to keep this standoff from turning into a massacre."

"I'm sorry, Rachel, but nobody came to Mount Carmel to follow your dad. They're not going to listen to him, even if he is David's right hand."

"They'll listen if David's incapacitated."

The words seemed to hang over Rachel in thin wisps of frozen breath.

"Incapacitated?"

"My dad's worked out a secret deal with the FBI. That's why he's been pushing David to meet with an outside mediator. The

Feds have got some kind of drug that will knock David out for days. The meeting's just an excuse to get it to Dad."

"You're going to drug David?"

"Into a coma, yeah."

My plan with Marshal seemed like small potatoes by comparison. As crazy as it sounded, drugging David might just work. Instead of selling out the whole of Mount Carmel as evil, we'd just be selling out David. The thought still didn't sit well with me. He might be nutty in the religion department and way too fond of my mom, but he wasn't a monster.

"So why do you need me to stay?" I asked.

"David listens to you. And we need you to keep him from calling this standoff the end of the world. If people think this is literally the End of Days, they won't leave him, no matter what. If this is just a dispute with the government and David's in a coma, Dad will be able to lead them out."

She was right. If the congregation heard half of what David was saying about the outbreak in Mexico, they'd dig in their heels until the bitter end. Still, I had no faith in my ability to convince David of anything. Liam's plan was dangerous, but so was Marshal's. Stay and risk everything to save a place I hated, or escape by selling everyone out.

"I have to stay," she said. "My dad needs me ... and I need you."

"You could have told me all this upstairs. Marshal, too. Why down here? Why risk getting caught?"

"Because you're right. There are tanks out there. And this isn't a game." She edged closer. "I wanted to be alone ... with you. I know I go on and on like I've done everything under the sun, but it's not true. I was going to wait for us to run away together. I was saving myself."

She took my hand. I could feel her trembling as she guided it inside her jacket. Maybe I was the one shaking. I don't know. I leaned into her lips with every ounce of my heart and suddenly the bus wasn't so cold. She was my choice. And if that meant staying here and saving everyone at Mount Carmel, that's exactly what I would do.

PART FOUR

Gather ye rosebuds while ye may,
Old Time is still a-flying,
And this same flower that smiles today
Tomorrow will be dying.

Robert Herrick

PSYWAR

I'D LIKE TO SAY THE EVENING WENT JUST LIKE RACHEL PLANNED, but our mad dash to ravage each other came to an abrupt halt when the FBI started blaring the sound of animals being slaughtered over giant loudspeakers outside the church. The shrieking death rattles did more than just derail our enthusiasm for each other. They woke up the entire congregation.

We scrambled for our clothes and raced to get upstairs before anyone missed us. The overlapping sounds of screeching animals became even more disorienting when the FBI cut power to the church. Oliver waited for us on the other side of the trapdoor. Climbing back into the main hall, I could see half a dozen people with flashlights scrambling for the cafeteria. Thankfully, none of them saw us.

The FBI must have leveled massive spotlights on the church because light poured in through the tiniest gaps in our boarded up windows. Strange shadows danced up and down the main hall as the FBI moved the lights into position.

"Get in the vault," Oliver ordered. "They're going to attack any second."

We ran for the cafeteria. I could hear Oliver slam the trapdoor shut behind us and bolt it in place. I tried to calm myself with the notion that it would take an army to get through that trapdoor. Then I remembered the FBI had brought an army.

Marshal waited for us near the entrance to the vault, disoriented and scared. We crammed inside with everyone else, expecting a quick assault on the church. We couldn't close the door all the way—the vault had no ventilation system—but the concrete walls did muffle the blaring loudspeakers enough to quell a mass panic attack.

Rachel and a few others had flashlights. The congregation settled in, huddling under these tiny islands of light in silent prayer. I held Rachel and Marshal as tight as I could. None of us spoke. We held our breath and waited for the sound of the gunfire that would end our lives.

It never came.

Everyone expected a quick assault, but as the hours passed, it became clear the only thing the FBI planned on attacking was our sleep. Rodney let us out of the vault sometime just before dawn. By then we were all sleep-deprived zombies. The recorded sounds of slaughter continued for days. Only the vault dampened the maddening noise.

Eventually, Liam set up a rotating sleep schedule and Marshal found a stash of firing-range earplugs to end the madness. Mom duct taped the church's supply of shower curtains together around the entrance to the vault, creating a makeshift airlock between it and the rest of the church. Protection from tear gas, she said. I had a hard time imagining the government using chemical weapons on a church, but after the helicopters and tanks and snipers, I had to admit nothing would seem out of bounds.

David and Liam had built the majority of Mount Carmel using material scavenged from more than a dozen of the free-standing Davidian houses that occupied the land before they took over. With the power off, the bitter winter winds savaged the poorly insulated church, turning it into an icebox.

We had half a dozen kerosene heaters. Two were placed in the vault, another two gave the chapel modest warmth, one heater went to David's room, and one to the bathroom. I dug out my black leather jacket, put it on over my gray hoodie, and tried my best to adjust to the new normal.

For the better part of a week, the FBI continued provoking us. After moving the press two miles back for "safety" reasons, they bulldozed the lot around the church, drove a tank over David's prized 1968 Camaro, and shot Jed Marsden dead when he tried to sneak back to the church from town. We all knew Jed was just trying to get back to his wife. He was in the middle of pulling a double shift when the FBI surrounded the church. The FBI told David and Liam that he had an assault rifle and fired first, but we all knew Jed had never fired more than a handgun in his life.

If that didn't raise tensions enough, the emergency crank radio, which now functioned as our only dependable source of outside information, reported chaos in Mexico as their outbreak turned into an epidemic. The virus, initially mistaken for meningitis, prompted deadly violence wherever it spread. The local radio station, KRLD, bounced between coverage of our standoff and the militarization of the border. True to the CDC's word, the number of cases in Texas didn't rise, but everyone on the radio seemed nervous they might.

As promised, I kept the rest of the teens in line. David was right. Two of Mount Carmel's most devout, Sarah and Noah, came to me with an idiotic escape plan. It didn't take much to convince them they were going to get themselves killed. The fact that Marshal, Rachel, and I stayed went a long way toward persuading the rest to do the same.

As each frigid day passed, I expected David to proclaim the outbreak in Mexico to be a sign from God, but he didn't. I couldn't understand why David listened to me, but I was thankful he did. The FBI seemed to get more erratic with each new day, and it didn't take long for even Marshal to concede that his plan probably would have landed us in a pine box or jail.

Whatever deal Liam had struck with the Feds, it became clear the government was divided over what to do with us. It took Liam a full week of negotiating to get the loudspeakers turned off and the power restored. In exchange for this gesture of goodwill, Liam got David to agree to meet with an outside group that included law enforcement to resolve the standoff. Up to that point, David had been holding out for news media.

The local sheriff, Tom Reynolds, and David's old defense attorney, Bud Rodriquez, were given permission to enter the church and mediate the standoff. David trusted Tom, who had handled previous disputes in a fair-minded way. And in the small town of Waco, David counted Bud as one of his drinking buddies.

David didn't know that Bud now worked for the FBI and would be delivering the drug to Liam. How Bud planned to pull this off, Rachel didn't know. She only knew her father had promised to wait until the day after the meeting to avoid any suspicion that the two events were linked.

I spent more and more time with David, acting as his gopher and offering up opinions when he asked, which was often. In fact, the more out of it he seemed, the more he relied on my opinion.

I finally got up the courage to ask—why me? Why not Liam or Oliver or Geoff or one of the other men? He just smiled that good ol' boy smile of his, adjusted his thick prescription glasses, and said, "Your mind isn't clouded by the belief that I'm infallible."

Then he leaned back against the bedroom wall that had held him upright the entire night, adjusting himself in a vain effort to find a more comfortable position for his gunshot wounds. "The world doesn't end with the apocalypse, Cyrus. It just changes." He closed his eyes and took a shallow breath. "You're an important part of that change, more than you know."

"I'm just a kid. How could I matter in all this?"

A fatherly smile worked its way through the pain. "The universe reveals itself in God's time, not man's. Speaking of which, I've got a little project for you."

The clock above his head read 6 a.m.

"It's early," I said. "Too early."

"I've been thinking. Tom and Bud are solid guys. They'll see our side of things. But they're going to have to go back and plead our case to the FBI and the public."

"Yeah."

"It would be better for us if they could take something with them to show the outside world we're not a bunch of loony tunes or satanic cultists. I was thinking maybe you could dig up the VHS camera, use it to tape Bible study, and interview some of the congregation."

"Me? I wouldn't know what to ask."

"Just ask them to tell their stories. Why they came here. What their lives are like. Why they don't want to leave. If people see that we're just ordinary folks, like them, they'll start questioning why the FBI needs to point tanks at a church."

I had to admit it was a good idea. I wasn't sure why David wanted me to do it. It's not like a VHS camera is difficult to operate. Press the red button and shoot. Was he trying to get rid of me?

"Some of the girls will already be up with the babies. Start with them."

"You don't want to go first?" I asked.

"Me? God, no. The way these FBI guys talk your ears off, I'm sick of the sound of my own voice."

"They're going to want to see you, though. They think you're some kind of monster."

"I tell you what. You go and interview some folks downstairs. We'll get the kids together this afternoon. You can tape me being a proud papa, introducing them to the world. Something normal like that." David arched his back and grimaced. "Send your mom around if you don't mind. I need to talk to her."

I hesitated.

"Go on, now. You've got work to do. I'll be fine."

TESTIMONY

DAVID DIDN'T TELL ME WHO TO INTERVIEW FIRST, AND I DIDN'T have to ask. I knew he would want me to start with his fourth wife, Jennifer. I found her sipping decaf in the corner of the kitchen while newborn Caleb Koresh nursed under a blanket. Despite the early hour, the cold, and the lack of running water, Jen looked like she had spent the past hour primping in front of a mirror. Her long blond hair, draped over her right shoulder, wouldn't have been out of place in a magazine ad. Only the dark circles under her eyes and her bandaged right hand hinted at a different story.

I told her David wanted me to tape people talking about their lives and why they came to Mount Carmel. She nodded and smiled, like I was making the most natural of requests, then suggested we tape it in the sitting room just off the main entrance.

By the time I grabbed the camera and extension cord out of storage, she had already made her way to the floral print, high-backed chair that sat next to an equally ugly couch. She had on a thick blue sweater with white snowflakes, the kind I imagined they'd sell near the ski slopes in Colorado.

A painting of Jerusalem at twilight hung behind her with two prominent bullet holes in it. Looking at the painting, I couldn't decide if the sun was rising or falling, a new beginning filled with hope and promise or a descent into darkness and despair. Maybe the artist intended both.

Jen rested Caleb in her lap and began removing the bandages on her hand while I plugged in the camera and inserted a fresh videotape. She must have noticed the look on my face because she stopped unwinding the gauze for a second.

"People should see what the ATF did to me," she said.

I hit record and tested the playback to make sure the camera worked before zooming in on Jen and Caleb. The record light flashed red, and I asked her if she was ready.

"You sure you're recording?" she asked.

"As long as you see the red light flashing, I'm recording. Just look at me when you talk." Marshal and I had played with the camera enough to know that much. "Pretend the camera doesn't exist."

"Okay." She seemed uncertain how to hold herself. I could see her wanting to reposition Caleb without putting any pressure on her exposed right hand. "My name is Jennifer Brenner."

She cleared her throat and smiled the kind of smile that only a former prom queen could muster. I could tell she wanted to say her last name was Koresh but knew the outside world wouldn't understand.

"I've been living here at Mount Carmel Church for ... I don't know—the past five years. I'm originally from New York. I came here of my own free will. I guess I should say that much. Bible study brought me here. My family raised me Christian in the Seventh Day Adventist church. They encouraged me to be close to Jesus and help people in need."

"Is that how you met David?" I asked, uncertain when or if I should insert myself into these interviews. I almost stopped myself from asking, but David seemed to think I would know what to do.

"I met Liam first. We were building a house together through Habitat for Humanity. He had been traveling on mission work and offered to help our church frame a detached pole barn. For a lawyer, he was pretty good with a hammer.

"Liam and I got to talking over lunch. I'm not usually that interested in traveling missionaries, they're full of blind faith and can't walk the talk in the real world, if you know what I mean, but Liam was different. He cared about his daughter, helping people, and the Bible—in that order. My family had him over for dinner a couple of times, and he told us about David and Mount Carmel and the Seven Seals of Revelation. It was interesting stuff."

"So you decided to move to Texas and study?" I asked.

"Gosh, no. I was nineteen and had just lost my husband to the war in Iraq. We had Liam over for dinner, that's all. We did exchange letters after that. His wife had died, and I think he felt pretty lonely. He knew I understood. Anyway, David came through our area about a year or so later, and I convinced my dad to let him stay at our house."

"What did you think of David when you met him?"

"Honestly?" Jen blushed. "I was disappointed. The way Liam talked him up, I expected somebody grand and confident. He kind of had this long, shaggy hair. And he was real quiet, you know, in that awkward kind of way of his. I thought he'd be preaching up a storm, but he just offered to talk about the Bible, try to answer any questions we had. He didn't act like he was anybody important."

"So why did you decide to go to Mount Carmel?"

"David invited our whole family out that summer. Dad couldn't get off work, but Mom and I went, you know. And I was so impressed. Not just with the depth of the Bible study, we met three times a day, but also the way people here lived the Scriptures. It's the only place I've ever been that knew how to walk the talk in the real world. Even now, with all these tanks and guns pointed at us, we're still having our Bible study, still praying God will grant us and the men outside the wisdom to resolve the misunderstandings and lies that have us trapped here."

"Do you feel like you can't leave?" I asked, adjusting the weight of the camera on my shoulder. After only a few minutes, I wished I had scouted up the tripod. "The news is saying that David's keeping us here against our will."

"I feel trapped by the FBI, if that's what you mean. I was free to go when and where I pleased before they showed up. Now, I'm scared for my family and my church's safety." She pulled Caleb tight, rocking him in her arms. "They've parked tanks in my front yard. Tanks. They've murdered unarmed members of my church. They nearly killed me and my boy. And all the while, they keep talking on TV about how we ambushed them. We didn't show up to their house in body armor, shooting at innocent women and children."

I tried to zoom the camera in on her disfigured right hand. The crooked index finger had swollen to twice its normal size and turned a dangerous looking purple.

"What happened to your hand?" I asked.

"I was nursing Caleb. Normally, I'm up before the crack of dawn, but he's been colicky lately, up at all hours. That's just the way of things with newborns. I guess it was about seven when the shooting started. Before I could get to the floor, bullets started flying in my upstairs window. One hit me here in the finger and then went through my shoulder right here. Whoever shot me didn't look long enough to notice that there was only an unarmed mother nursing her baby in the room."

"What did you do?"

"I dropped to the ground, wrapped my arms tight around Caleb, and tried to get under the bed. But one of those armored ATF guys came through my window shooting his rifle as quick as he could pull the trigger. I kept screaming, 'I surrender!' He didn't hear me, or he didn't care.

"You know," she paused as if thinking back through the moment, "he didn't even have a walkie-talkie or anything. My room's on the backside of the church, about as far away from the front door as you can get. David could've given up on the spot and they would've had no way of telling him. If you ask me, they planned to shoot their way into our church whether we surrendered or not. I'm one of the lucky ones. They threw grenades into some rooms."

The reality of what had happened was starting to get to Jen. Her eyes welled up and tears flowed down her cheeks. She didn't reach for a tissue on the side table, though; she let the tears fall. Caleb started crying with her and she stopped herself long enough to comfort him.

"If, by some miracle, people are watching this tape, you've been told a bunch of lies about us to justify what the ATF did here. We're a church. Our members are lawyers and college professors and nurses and everyday people living and studying the Christian Bible together. We're scared for our lives in here, afraid they're going to kill us to cover up the truth about what they did."

I started to put the camera down, but Jen motioned for me to wait.

"I shouldn't let them get to me, I know. Jesus told us to love our enemies. But I cannot conscience the lies the FBI is telling about us on television. We're a church, not some kind of military target. And I'm here of my own free will. All this talk about mind control and cults would be laughable if people didn't take it seriously. If you're watching this, please help us get the press in here so they can reveal the truth."

"Anything else you'd like to add?"

"Just hello to my mom and dad, my family. I love you all and can't wait to introduce you to Caleb."

I shut off the camera, sitting it on the couch and stretching my shoulder. Jen asked me to take Caleb while she rewrapped her hand.

The interviews continued all afternoon. After a while, they all sounded the same to me. Everyone wanted to make it clear that they were normal and here of their own free will. And each person had some aspect of the ATF's story that they felt the need to argue.

After dinner, I filmed David putting each of his kids on his lap. He even joked that they should use their situation to demand ice cream from the hostage negotiators. I managed to avoid my fifteen minutes of fame by insisting I stay behind the camera. David looked horrible in his sweat and bloodstained tank top, but he came across as a proud papa. He even made a point of thanking me for working so hard to tape everyone's stories.

When we got to the last kid, newborn Caleb, I asked David if there was anything he wanted to say to people out there in the world. He rubbed his stubble for a minute like he wasn't sure if it would help or not.

"You've all been hearing way too much about me, and I doubt you'd believe anything I have to say, seeing how the FBI's painted me to be the Devil. I'd just ask you to please listen to our stories and ask yourself if we sound all that different from the good folks at your own church. We didn't ask for any of this."

David couldn't have found a better note to leave things on. I wish I had shut off the camera right then, but I didn't. As soon as Jen lifted Caleb out of David's arms, his face changed. You could see the exhaustion and pain turn to defiance.

"I will say this to the ATF. You got an argument with me, you come and argue with me. But you come pointing guns at my wives and my kids, dammit, I'll meet you at the door anytime. And I'm sorry some of your guys got shot, but, hey, God will have to sort that out, won't he."

I shut the camera off before he could get himself any more riled up and told myself that I'd erase that last bit before we handed it over to the sheriff and Bud.

PART FIVE

A lie gets halfway around the world
before the truth has a chance to get its pants on.

Winston Churchill

TIPPING POINT

GETTING DAVID READY FOR HIS TWO O'CLOCK MEETING WITH the negotiators took more effort than I expected. I practically had to hold him up as he changed shirts. Whatever medication Mom was giving him, it wasn't working. Even with my support, he moved in slow motion, grunting in pain as his muscles pulled around his chest wound.

"How much time do we have?" he asked.

"About fifteen minutes."

David nodded as if I'd just handed him a list of chores after a long day at work. He closed his eyes and took a deep breath, buttoning his light brown dress shirt over the tight bandage that crisscrossed his midsection. "We'll get there," he muttered and then repeated, as if trying to convince himself.

"You won't have to come back upstairs," I promised. "The old leather couch in Liam's office has your name on it."

We hobbled to the door, arm in arm. Oliver waited outside with my mom. Her disapproving stares had been replaced by something that almost resembled pride. I couldn't help but shrink from her gaze. I wasn't saving her beloved husband, at least not in a way that would meet with her approval. She would disown me when she found out the truth.

Oliver shouldered David's other side and together we carried him downstairs. We rested at the bottom of the steps and again in the chapel, where David said a short prayer. Liam waited for us in his office, just off the telephone room. The wood-paneled walls, which hid any number of structural problems, sported legal certificates from the universities of Edinburgh and Oxford, alongside pictures of trips to India and Jerusalem. He wore one of his dark blue lawyer suits.

Rachel sat to his side in a cafeteria chair. She looked like a court stenographer with her black skirt, yellow sweater, and notepad. She wore her hair up, exposing her pale, slender neck.

"They're on their way over," Liam said. He cleared a pile of old paperwork off the room's worn leather couch and piled it on his ever-present puzzle table. "Cyrus, can you get us a pitcher of tap water and some glasses?"

I helped David sit down on the couch and then headed to the kitchen next door. Rodney had managed to use a makeshift hand pump to restore a minor supply of water. Not enough to take a shower, but enough to keep us from dying of dehydration. Bringing the tray back to Liam's office, I saw Oliver showing Sheriff Reynolds and Bud the front door. The sheriff seemed keenly interested in the bullet holes. I watched Bud take a few pictures before I ducked back into Liam's office.

I set the pitcher of water on the desk and poured David a glass, taking my place at his side. If Marshal had been in the room, looking at Rachel in her business skirt and me cozying up to David, he would have laughed us out of the church. Oliver knocked on the door before entering with the sheriff and Bud.

The first thing I noticed, the sheriff entered the room with his sidearm. He kept it holstered, but it was still there. Apparently, David had insisted the sheriff come in as he would have if half the FBI wasn't camped on our doorstep.

"Ma'am," the sheriff said, tipping what looked to be a new

Stetson in deference to Rachel. I could see her biting back the urge to tip an imaginary hat, lower her voice, and say something silly back.

Sheriff Reynolds turned his attention to the couch, extending his hand. "David, old buddy, you're not looking so good."

"I look better than I feel. How you holding up, Tom?"

"I'd be a good deal better without all these yahoos mucking up my town. What you say we kick 'em all out and settle this like men?" The sheriff grinned and took a seat across from David, motioning for Bud to do the same.

"So sorry about everything," Bud said, nervously shaking David's and Liam's hands before taking a seat. "I wish I was here for a jam session."

David offered Bud a toothy grin. "You and your bass guitar are welcome any time."

Bud had dressed in his best suit, anticipating the media circus that would be hanging on his every word after this meeting. Only his thin-haired ponytail spoke of a man that preferred to knock back a few brews and play music.

"We do apologize for the inconvenience," Liam said. "Oliver, take their coats. Would either of you gentlemen like a glass of tap water? I'm afraid it's all we have to offer."

"Speaking of which," the sheriff interrupted, "I hope you don't mind, but I wheeled a whole dolly cart of fresh milk up to the front door. I'm sure you folks are running low."

"That's quite kind of you," Liam said. "Oliver, please get the milk to the mothers at once."

Oliver hung up the coats and left us so he could take care of the milk.

"We'd like to get you folks some medical treatment soon." The sheriff looked at me. "I'd hate to see you lose the rest of that ear to infection."

A long pause followed the comment, the six of us taking a moment to wrap our brains around the events that brought us to this point. Bud broke the silence, opening his briefcase and pulling out a small pile of blue folders. He handed one to each of us, even Rachel and me, and stowed the extras back in his briefcase.

"I hope you don't mind, David, but I took the liberty of putting together some paperwork on the charges against you and the church, so we can talk about the legal issues and such."

"Maybe we should set that aside for the moment," the sheriff said.

"I agree." David handed me his folder unopened, and I placed it on top of my own.

"I've been listening to the government's side of things nonstop for a week and a half," the sheriff said. "You boys want to tell me what the heck happened out here?"

"Honest to God, Tom." David scratched the back of his head. "Those ATF boys pulled up in long cattle trailers and started firing at us before they'd even identified themselves. I came out to see if we could talk things through and had to dive back inside to keep from getting shot. They killed poor Taylor Wilhelm in the doorway."

"The ATF says the holes in your door are from your people shooting out at them."

"Come on," David said. "One look at those doors and you know who was shooting at who. Besides, why would I ambush them by blindly firing through a solid metal door when I've got windows all around it in a perfect position to take them out?"

"Well ..." The sheriff took his brown Stetson off, bending the new brim in an attempt to train it to the shape of his old hat. "Judging by the look of your front door, I'd say the ATF is full of it."

The sheriff believed us. Everyone in the room breathed a sigh of relief.

"Of course, you boys understand that don't give you the right to shoot back at them."

"On that point," Liam said, "I have to disagree with you. Texas law allows a private citizen to return fire if the police shoot at them without identifying themselves. And the warrant the ATF obtained required them to knock on the front door and announce that—"

"Did you know they was law enforcement officers?" the sheriff asked. "When they pulled up in those cattle trailers, Liam. Did you know?"

Liam nodded.

"Then I don't want to hear any crap about you hiding behind Texas law. You knowingly fired on law enforcement. There wasn't any misunderstanding. You knew what you were doing, and somebody's going to have to pay for that."

David looked the sheriff up and down. The silence between them seemed to last forever. Just when I thought things might take a turn for the worse, David nodded and said, "Fair enough."

I didn't realize it until the words were halfway out of my mouth, but I wasn't in any mood to retreat.

"What about them?" I asked. "Are they going to pay for shooting Nick or Taylor or Mrs. Jankis? The ATF had guys living in the farmhouse across the street from us for months. They've been over here for dinner, waved to David every day when he jogged past. They could have arrested him while he ran or when he went to town or when we played a gig. Why storm a church with a small army when you don't have to?"

"I wish I had a good answer for you, Cyrus," the sheriff said. "This whole thing doesn't pass the smell test. It's like some giant publicity stunt gone wrong. I told 'em to let me come down here and pick him up myself, but they weren't having any of it."

I couldn't help but wonder if David would have gone with the sheriff. My gut told me he would have surrendered without a fight. A lone squad car investigating a criminal complaint didn't exactly scream forces of Babylon attacking the way the ATF's shock-and-awe raid did.

"So how do we get out of this mess?" David asked. "I mean, contrary to the popular belief on television, I don't want my people dying over me."

"That's good to hear," the sheriff said. "The Feds have been telling us you think you're Jesus Christ."

Another awkward pause. David shook his head and reached for his water. "You don't believe any of that, do you?"

"I'm not sure what to believe." The sheriff smiled, but it looked forced. "You've been a good neighbor to the folks in Waco. I've got no complaints, but you keep to yourself out here. Nobody's really sure what you're worshiping or what you believe."

"Well, I appreciate your honesty." David unconsciously brought his right arm up to his chest wound. "I've been teaching the gospel out here for four years now. The same Christian book you've been reading every Sunday in town. And I've never said I was Jesus Christ. Not once. The only claim I've ever made is that God anointed me."

"I don't know," the sheriff said, "it sounds an awful lot like you're saying you're—"

"God anointed Noah and Moses and King Cyrus and Jesus and a whole host of others. When I say 'anointed,' I simply mean given a mission from God. Catholics believe the Pope is anointed. Joseph Smith believed he was anointed when he started the Mormon Church. TV evangelists won't shut up about their mission from God. How can they be allowed to have one, but you've got to park tanks on my lawn because I do?"

David winced as he shifted his weight, not wanting the pain to interfere with his train of thought. "In 1985, I stood at the Temple Mount in Jerusalem and received a vision about the Bible, about a message in the Good Book that could save humanity. I came here to teach that message, and it's drawn biblical scholars from around the world. This isn't some kind of crazy cult."

"Calm down, David." The sheriff's voice softened to a whisper. "Nobody here that knows you is calling this a cult."

"And none of you are getting on TV to defend us either."

"You're right," the sheriff said as he continued to train his hat, his head hung low, "but we're here now, aren't we, trying to help you sort this out?"

"And we talked the FBI into stopping that psychological warfare nonsense," Bud said.

"For now," the sheriff added. "If we can't figure out a way to resolve this ridiculous standoff ... well, I'm not sure what they're going to do next."

"If they think I'm so unstable," David said, "if they think we're all crazy in here, why would they try to deprive us of sleep? Didn't anyone tell them lack of sleep makes people erratic?"

"I did," Bud said, "but they've got this group of 'cult experts' telling them it's a good idea. As crazy as it sounds, they're talking about you using mind control over everyone, like the folks here can't think for themselves. The psywar stuff is supposed to disrupt your hold on them or some kind of crap like that. Doesn't make a lick of sense to me."

"Maybe now would be a good time to talk about the charges against David and the church," the sheriff said.

Bud opened his folder and motioned for the rest of us to do the same. Inside, next to a fresh pad of paper and pen, Bud had crammed a half-inch-thick stack of government documents. Looking at the expression on Liam's face as he opened his folder, I knew the drug had been delivered.

"The paperwork on the search warrant claims you're running a drug lab, stockpiling an armory of illegal weapons, and having sexual relationships with underage girls." Bud took a deep breath before continuing. "The shootings are a whole other mess."

David leaned forward, wincing in pain, and looked the sheriff straight in the eyes. "You think I'm running drugs and guns and abusing kids?"

"I don't, but these folks have a right, under the laws of Texas, to come in here and find that out for themselves. David, we've got to get past what is or isn't right about this situation. It's time to focus on how to resolve it before more people get hurt."

"Like Jed Marshal?" Rachel asked. She had so quietly occupied her corner of the room that the accusation startled Bud. "Your FBI says he pulled an assault rifle on them while he was trying to get back to the church, but that tottering old man's half-blind. And he's never fired more than a handgun in his life."

"They're not my FBI." The sheriff leaned forward, taking the time to make eye contact with each one of us. "I'm a lot more worried about what they're going to do than I am you folks. That's why we've got to put a stop to this, before they do something monumentally stupid. They want to put you people away for life. And I'm starting to think they don't care if that includes jail cells or cemeteries."

"That's the problem," Liam said. "They can't be impartial. I'm a guest in your country, and perhaps that means I have no right to speak my mind, but where I come from the government has a way of losing evidence that exposes their own wrongdoing."

"An independent examination of the facts, is that what you're thinking?" I watched Bud sit up straight. "We'd have to bar the ATF and FBI from the crime scene." He tilted his head back and forth, mulling the idea over. "If we got the news media involved, they might be able to force the government to accept the idea. Assuming it's your only demand?"

David reached for his water and took a long, slow drink. "I don't need any independent investigation."

The room stopped. I could tell David relished the control that came with everyone hanging on his next word. Maybe that's why he loved preaching so much. His grin passed, replaced by what seemed to be a more sober thought.

"I'm sorry, Cyrus." David gave my leg a fatherly pat. "I know you don't agree with me, but I owe this one to the world." David continued before I could stop him. "Those cable news folks tried to set up an interview with me, before the FBI cut our outside line. You get me an hour on CNN with old Larry King, and I'll lead everyone out of here peacefully. I'm not afraid of judgment, not the government's anyway. I just need to make sure my message gets to the people before it's too late."

Bud and the sheriff traded ominous looks.

"I don't understand," Bud said. "Too late for what?"

"Does it matter?" I interrupted. "If it ends this standoff, who cares?"

Bud started to say something, but the sheriff shushed him with a wave of his hand. "Son, if you folks are planning something here, I need to know about it. There are a lot of innocent people involved, and we don't need some kind of stunt to get everyone—"

"It's the epidemic," David said. "Down in Mexico. It's about to stop knocking on our door and kick the whole damn thing in. When that happens, the Second Seal will break, and the nonbelievers will be consumed by the wrath of God. If I can warn people, I might be able to save at least a few of them from the Fallen."

"The Fallen?" The alarm in the sheriff's voice was palpable.

"The infected remnants of the human race," David replied.

"Now, David," Bud said, trying to rescue the fragile negotiation. "I think we were on firmer ground talking about an independent investigation. We can get you a camera to tape your message or a book deal after—"

"Actually," I interrupted, trying to wrestle the conversation away from David's Bible nonsense, "I made a tape of church members sharing their stories, explaining why they've come here and what life's like inside the church."

Liam grabbed the tape off a stack of papers on his desk and handed it to Bud.

"If people could see this," I said, "they'd know the government was lying about us."

"I know I told you to make the tape, Cyrus, but the more I think about it, the more I think it's too late for that sort of thing." David shook his head in disgust. "I should have seen this coming sooner. I should've spent more time traveling with the message instead of making people come to me."

David looked around the room, realizing that he'd lost the sheriff and Bud.

"Listen, you don't believe. That's fine. Get me the time anyway. Let me say my piece and face judgment. If the world thinks I'm crazy, if I can't save anyone ... at least I'll know I tried. You're good men for coming out here and standing up for us. Get us an independent investigation, so they don't think I'm nuts, and an hour with the cable news folks. You do both and you have my word we'll all surrender peaceful-like. No stunts."

The sheriff put on his hat, standing.

"What about the charges?" Bud said. "We still have a lot to go through."

"This man's made up his mind," the sheriff said. "You need to learn to respect that."

WE INTERRUPT THIS PROGRAM

I CAUGHT UP WITH MARSHAL AN HOUR LATER IN THE GUN ROOM. He had disassembled a rusted, lever-action rifle and was in the process of cleaning and transferring the firing mechanism to another stock. David didn't let him fire the rifles, but given his knack for cleaning and repairing them, he let Marshal earn his keep by helping to recondition them from spare parts. Most sold at the gun shows for a tidy profit.

The room had been nearly emptied the morning before the raid for a gun show in Austin. When the ATF fought their way into the room, I'm sure the lack of weapons surprised them. Only half a dozen pistols and non-functioning rifles remained. Hardly the vast armory they imagined. If they imagined it at all. Liam and David seemed to think the drug and gun charges were just trumped up to use a loophole in something called the Commitatus Act to get the military involved in the raid. Of course, they were mum when it came to the charge that David had slept with underage girls.

Without looking up from the lever mechanism he was cleaning, Marshal asked me how it went.

"Complete disaster," I said. "The sheriff came to us, literally hat in hand, looking for a way out of this mess. You could tell he felt horrible for not finding a way to stop the raid."

"So how did David screw it up?"

"By asking for an hour on national TV to save as many souls as he could. You should've seen the look on the sheriff's face when David started talking about Mexico and the end of the world, flushed any chance we had of negotiating our way out of here."

"So what's David offering them in exchange for his sixty minutes of fame?"

"He says he'll lead us all out of the church, unarmed."

"Do you think that'll happen?"

I hadn't thought about it. David had repeatedly told me that God would protect the true believers from His wrath, but what did that mean? According to his teachings, the Third and Fourth Seals came shortly after the Second, bringing an unfair bargain and then death to his followers. Sure, there was the promise of resurrection three years later, as the Seals continued to break, but this battle was never meant to be won.

"Cyrus, what do you think he's going to do?"

"I don't know."

"What about Rachel's plan?" he whispered, looking back at the open doorway.

I walked to the hallway to check for prying ears before answering. The room's door had long since been removed to patch a hole in the floor or cover up a window.

"From the look on Liam's face, I'd say Bud made the delivery, but I don't know for sure."

"If he did," Marshal reassembled the second rifle with the borrowed part, "we'll be out of here tomorrow, one way or the other."

He had a point, but I still felt uneasy about the prospect of putting David in a coma. What if he died? I'd be just as responsible as Liam for killing him. I wasn't sure if I could live with that. Then again, if we didn't do it, odds were against us living. Period.

"We need to come up with a plan for how we're going to find

each other, after they split us up, I mean. What about your dad? Is he still working for the government up in Sulphur Springs?"

"He's still working at the resort, if that's what you mean. You're not supposed to know more than that."

"What? We're going to end up in more trouble?"

"Just drop it," I said. "I shouldn't have told you anything about The Greenbrier."

"Do you think he'll try to get custody if we get out of here?"

"I don't know. He tried to, you know, after—" I couldn't bring myself to say Michael's name out loud. "But that was before I called him a backstabbing coward for marrying Melanie."

"Yeah, his wedding day probably wasn't the place for that."

"Total train wreck."

"What if we just met up at his house? Or at least kept him up on wherever we were hiding, so we could find each other through him." He looked up from his work. "Do you think your dad would at least help us stay together?"

"He thinks Mom's bat-shit crazy," I said. "I think he'd take me in before he'd let a foster home ruin me. If I could explain things. If he understood the three of us were family, I think he'd help us. But West Virginia's a long ways from Texas."

"The further, the better, if you ask me. We're going to need to memorize his address. CPS can't know what we're planning."

"CPS?"

"Child Protective Services. Our first stop if they don't throw us in jail."

"What about your dad?" I asked. "Any idea what he'll do?"

Marshal went back to work on the gun. "I'll find a way out of that mess. I always do. He might be back in jail. He might not even claim me. Who knows?"

"I should get back before David misses me."

"What are you supposed to be doing?"

"Taking a dump." I half smiled. "You think he's going to check on me?"

"Be careful. It won't take much for David to decide you're not trustworthy. Things could get super paranoid between now and tomorrow."

I walked down the deserted long hall. With the women and children living in the vault, an eerie calm had settled over the upstairs. Doors missing. Windows boarded up. Closet doors nailed over holes in the floor. I yelped when an arm reached out of one of the doorways and pulled me into a dark room.

Before I could react, I was up against a wall with a tongue in my mouth. A hint of lavender accompanied Rachel's lips. My arms reached for her waist and I pulled her as close to me as I could without ripping her jeans clean off. She stifled a giggle, giving me a few lingering kisses before pulling away.

"Right, now that we've got that settled proper," she said, "I need to get down to the chapel." She darted out of the room, changing course after she realized she was going the wrong way. "You scream like a girl," she said, giggling down the hallway.

I took a minute to compose myself. It wouldn't do for me to walk back to Liam's office sporting a woody with his daughter's name on it. I turned the room's light on and checked my lips in the mirror on the wall. No lipstick. I saw Mrs. Henderson's robe hanging beside the mirror and couldn't help but laugh. This room had just seen more action in one minute than it had in all the time since she moved to Mount Carmel.

Concern replaced the spring in my step as I neared Liam's office. I could hear the sheriff and Bud on the conference call line with a third voice that sounded familiar. As I got closer, I recognized the hostage negotiator's voice from the call in David's bedroom. Shepherd was his name.

Liam paced behind his desk while David occupied the same spot I'd left him in. "What do you mean they can't get me time on CNN?" David asked. "The folks at Larry King begged us for an interview. Are you trying to tell me that all the sudden they got no interest?"

"I'm not saying that, David." Shepherd's relaxed tone seemed forced.

"Then what are you saying?" Liam asked.

"After discussing your demands with the powers that be, the FBI has decided to go along with an independent investigation."

"And what about my interview?"

"For reasons that have nothing to do with your situation in Waco, the FBI can't allow you to go on national television. It's not the right time for that."

"Why not now? Or as I surrender, if they're worried I'm not a man of my word."

"Sheriff Reynolds here. I know these people haven't been straight with you on a lot of stuff, David, but there's things happening on the border that haven't hit the TV yet. The government can't have you making a bad situation worse by spreading panic. Now we both know an independent investigation is going to reveal the truth on both sides. Outside of the boys that shot ATF agents, who you and I both know deserve to go to jail, everyone else will be cleared. You have to think about your children and the future of your ministry."

"I've seen the future," David replied. "I need a platform big enough to save as many as I can before the Fallen sweep across—"

"Sheriff," I interrupted, "what's happening on the border?"

The better part of a minute went by without a response. We all traded ominous glances. I held my breath, hoping for an answer different than the one David would give.

"The epidemic has infected parts of the military along the border," Agent Shepherd finally offered. "Some units are attacking each other and anyone else that gets in their way. The FBI has been ordered to get you under control so they can be reassigned. The White House is considering martial law."

"Which is exactly why you need to get me on television." David raised his arms to the speakerphone in frustration. "I can save people."

"You mean you can scare the pants off them," Shepherd replied. "I'm all for you having your say and then turning yourself in, don't get me wrong, but putting you on TV would be like throwing gasoline on a ..."

The agent's voice trailed off. I could hear someone in the distant background yelling, "It's happening! It's really happening!"

Just then, the phone line went dead. I don't know what scared me more. Fear of the unknown, or fear that David might actually know what he's talking about. For the first time since my mom dragged me to this rat-infested hole in Texas, I had to face the possibility that David was, in fact, exactly who he said he was.

"Cyrus," Liam ordered, "get the telly from David's room!"

I scrambled upstairs, yelling for Marshal as I passed by the gun room.

"What's going on?" he asked.

I almost yanked the twelve-inch television out of the wall, stopping short when I realized it was still attached. Setting it on the floor, I unscrewed the coax, pulled the power plug, and carried it into the hallway with the cords dangling behind.

"Come on!" I yelled, running past Marshal and down the front steps. When I got back to the office, Liam was still futzing with the phone.

"Nothing," he said.

I plugged the TV in and turned it on, extending the rabbit ears. On the plains of Texas, you didn't need a big antenna to get crystal clear reception. But the local stations aired wall-to-wall game shows this time of day, and I had no idea where to plug in the coax.

"Cable outlet's behind the bookcase," Liam said.

Before he could get around his desk to help me, Marshal bounded into the room and pulled the bookcase out from the wall. I reached behind and started screwing the cable into the outlet. CNN started out fuzzy as I threaded the coax. When the static cleared, the sound of fighter jets replaced it.

"Holy shit!" the TV reporter said, ducking. The camera showed five F-15 Strike Eagles flying low over the reporter's head in a race for the edge of some border town. It looked like San Juan or maybe

Nuevo. The modest skyline of warehouses and shopping malls erupted in a series of explosions.

"Are you getting this?" she asked, off camera.

We heard more jets but couldn't see them. David started to speak but stopped himself as the footage froze and then looped back to the beginning.

"We're getting unconfirmed reports of outbreaks here in Mission, Texas," the reporter said, responding to a question from the unseen news anchor. She was a pale blond with big hair and bright red lipstick that matched her dress. "We haven't seen any evidence of the violence that has plagued Mexico, but this close to the border, people are getting nervous. And with good reason: For the past hour we've heard the distant thunder of American tanks firing into the Mexican desert. Military sources tell us the White House has given the 49th Armored Division approval to clear a buffer zone. Clear it of what, we can only speculate. The spokesman from the CDC I talked to cautioned against alarm, calling the military's move precautionary. For the moment, he said, this is still a Mexican prob—"

Low altitude jets once again screamed over her head.

"Holy—"

"That was Bobbie Battista in Mission, Texas. We're getting word that President Gore will be addressing the nation from the Oval Office within the next hour. And I'm told, following that coverage, an exclusive interview with Vice President Bill Clinton, currently in California on a fundraising trip. So stay with us. We'll have more developments from the border with Mexico right after this break."

An advertisement for mac and cheese replaced the news anchor. David looked fit to be tied. If he had the strength, I think he would have chucked his shoe at the small TV set. He looked to Liam, who had stopped trying to get the phone line back. "I need to talk to the FBI," he said.

"I cannot imagine what good that'll do," Liam replied.

"I saw this, in Jerusalem, when the angels came to me. The

President's going to carpet bomb the border, hoping to cauterize the wound, but the blasts are just going to help the epidemic spread."

Liam shot David a look like he was crazy before returning to the phone line.

"I have to warn them," David said to himself. "It's the right thing to do."

"Ye can't go out there! They'll shoot you!" Liam slammed the phone down in frustration.

"What do you think, Cyrus?" David waited for my response.

I looked to Liam and Marshal and then back to the TV. I couldn't wrap my brain around the idea that this was happening. Could David be the Seventh Messenger of Revelation, the Keeper of the Seals? This had to be a nightmare. It was too crazy to be true.

"Stop looking for answers from other people. What does your gut tell you?"

"Well." I turned back to David. "When the sheriff said the powers that be wouldn't let you give that interview, it didn't sound like he meant the FBI. I don't think talking to them will do you any good. And if you somehow are the Seventh Messenger, then this is the will of God. You can't stop it. We should see what the President has to say and make plans to keep everyone here safe."

David took his glasses off, rubbing his face as he considered my opinion. "Alright, Cyrus. Let's get everyone together in the chapel. We'll watch Gore's address on the big screen and see what happens from there."

PART SIX

Things fall apart; the centre cannot hold;
Mere anarchy is loosed upon the world,
The blood-dimmed tide is loosed, and everywhere
The ceremony of innocence is drowned;

Surely some revelation is at hand.

William Butler Yeats

BREAKING THE WORLD

I HELD RACHEL IN MY ARMS AS WE WATCHED THE PRESIDENT address the nation. If anyone in the church had a problem with that, they didn't speak up. The first thing we noticed was the back-drop of his address. Staged to look like the Oval Office, it had a flat appearance that time had yellowed. Even the desk didn't look right. The size of it didn't match the scale of the room.

"Good evening," President Gore began, his measured Virginian drawl as prominent as the dark circles under his eyes. "I come to you today from the Oval Office as America faces perhaps its greatest challenge since the Civil War threatened to tear our Union apart. As many of you know, there is a virus sweeping across Central America. Over the past twelve hours, infection rates have skyrocketed to unprecedented levels, spreading at a pace not seen in all of recorded human history. We have lost contact with the central government of Mexico and its neighbors to the south. Satellite imagery of the infected areas shows evidence of wide-spread civil unrest, looting, and in extreme cases, entire cities in flames."

President Gore brought his fingers around the paper copy of

the speech that rested on his desk. If I had to guess, I'd say he was giving the address from the safety of some undisclosed bunker.

More evidence David's visions were coming true.

"While our scientists at the CDC have successfully quarantined the half-dozen cases of this unknown virus in Texas, it is impossible to see the recent events in Mexico, Belize, and Guatemala as anything but canaries in the proverbial coal mine. Over the past two hours, I have received troubling reports that our military units along the southern border have become infected and are no longer under my direct control. To put it bluntly, we have already lost the great state of Texas."

The chapel filled with gasps, drowning out the emergency broadcast. I couldn't wrap my brain around the words. Lost Texas? What did he mean?

"Oi!" Rachel screamed at the congregation. Her booming voice echoed off the chapel walls, startling the entire church. "Everyone stuff it!"

"As your Commander-in-Chief, it is my solemn duty to protect the United States of America. Without a cure, that means containing the spread of this infection at all costs. Overnight, the Joint Chiefs drafted a failsafe plan that I have just put into action. Low-yield, tactical nuclear weapons will soon be detonated along the southern reaches of our great country, from Texas to California. They will create an uninhabitable buffer zone that will protect the United States from any further contamination from the south.

"I do not take the decision to use nuclear weapons on American soil lightly. And I would ask everyone in our great nation, regardless of religion, to pray for the brave men of our armed forces who will perish alongside the citizens they rushed to defend. Effective immediately, I am suspending all travel in the border states and declaring martial law.

"I leave you with the immortal words of Abraham Lincoln." The President closed his eyes and bowed his head, his voice breaking ever so slightly. "'With malice toward none, with charity for all, with firmness in the right as God gives us to see the right, let us strive on to finish the work we are in, to bind up the nation's wounds, to do all which may achieve and cherish a just and lasting peace among ourselves and with all nations.'"

He opened his eyes and looked back into the camera.

"May God bless all of you, and may God bless the United States of—"

The entire church rattled from the foundation up. Static replaced the image of President Gore's fake Oval Office. I ran to the front door with Rachel and Marshal following close behind. Before either of them could stop me, I kicked away the boards reinforcing the front entrance. I had to know if David was right. I threw open the door and looked to the south. Distant mushroom clouds blotted out the late-afternoon sky.

A second chain of blasts, this time much closer, lit up the southern horizon. Painful columns of light seared my eyes as they charged for the heavens. I stumbled backward, falling into the church as the violent tremors reached us. Mount Carmel shuddered, convulsing from multiple shock waves. I covered my head, expecting the whole building to collapse on top of me.

When I opened my eyes, the bright flashes of nuclear destruction remained superimposed over everything I looked at. Rachel helped me up while Marshal closed and reinforced the door. I blinked hard, but the columns of light refused to fade. Did I just watch Austin get wiped off the map? The news had reported cases that far north.

Turning back to the chapel, I saw David struggle across the stage and shut off the static-filled television. Rachel and Marshal helped me back to the chapel as he began to speak.

"Seven years ago, I stood in the center of Jerusalem, at the Temple Mount, and had a vision of this day. The time you've been waiting for is here." Despite my eyes, I could see the pain on David's face as he strained to stand before his congregation. "The Second Seal is broken. Those nukes won't stop the epidemic. They'll fuel it. Even now, as I speak, the fallout is spreading madness across the Southwest, converting the fallen souls of

Babylon into violent, psychotic slaves. In my vision, these fallen subjects of The Great Deceiver devour everything and everyone within their increasing grasp, making their victims forever unclean in the eyes of God."

David clutched his midsection, his knees almost buckling under the strain of standing. Rachel reached for my hand, holding it so tight her knuckles turned white. Would her father still poison David? Or would he accept the truth of his prophecy? Both possibilities scared the hell out of me.

"You all know," David continued, reaching for the podium to steady himself, "there is a special place in heaven for His chosen. I had hoped to speak on national television, to convert a few more souls before Judgment Day. I'm sad to say I have not lived up to God's plan for me. I've only saved a small hamlet. Which is why I'm gonna ask something of you, something difficult to give."

Again, David paused. Whether out of pain or purposeful affect, he took a deep breath and waited for us all to lean forward.

"Outside our church, the men who attacked us, who tried to kill our families, sit helpless in the face of certain doom. I would like to invite them to throw down their arms and take refuge in our church. I'd like to offer them the same protection God has granted us."

The congregation responded to David's plea with silence. His followers bowed their heads in shame, unable to forgive their accusers.

"They slaughtered innocent members of our family," my mom said, breaking the silence. "They almost killed you. How can you offer them sanctuary?"

David motioned for Rachel's dad to bring him a chair. Liam raced over, holding it steady as David slumped into it.

"I have saved so few. In God's eyes, I fear, not enough. It is a difficult thing I ask, I know, but there is room in God's heart for those men and women who would choose my house over the world now. Don't forget the parable of the lost son. You have been dutiful servants and His house is already yours. But outside, your lost brothers and sisters wander beyond the boundaries of His love. They still have a chance. I can't think of a better way to enter the Kingdom of God than by offering your enemy one last chance at salvation."

Resting his elbows on his knees, David looked out across his followers.

"The hour of man is late and time is short. There are many preparations to make before the Fallen reach Mount Carmel. I ask you now to stand if you can accept one last attempt to bring your lost brothers and sisters into God's home."

Marshal surprised me by being the first to stand. I had been so confused by the apparent fulfillment of David's prophecies that I never considered their impact on him or Rachel. Mrs. Davies and Rodney stood with Marshal. Soon three became half the room, and then half became the entire congregation. I stood with Rachel at the very end, not wanting to be further outcast.

"We will try to save them one last time," David said, his voice regaining a small bit of its lost strength.

It took Marshal and me a few minutes to get David back to Liam's office. The phone line was still dead and we couldn't find a television station. Rachel fetched the crank radio and we travelled up and down the dial.

Nothing.

If not for the FBI siege, we would have felt like the last people on Earth. David settled back into his couch, worse for his trip to the chapel. His skin had turned a pale yellow. I couldn't help but wonder if he would last long enough to be poisoned. I traded glances with Liam, who seemed to be thinking the same thing. The nuclear flashes had faded enough for me to believe they would soon go away, but they still cast everyone I looked at in a series of vertical explosions. Austin was at least two hours away by car. I couldn't imagine what the blasts would have done to my eyes if we'd been closer.

"Should we send Oliver," Liam asked David, "or someone without a family?"

"I'll go," Marshal offered, again surprising me.

"Half a chance they'll be shooting at whoever we send out," David said. "You know I can't—"

"I'll be okay. It's important."

"Marshall—" I started to raise my voice, to tell him he needed to take a step back from the crazy train, but David interrupted me.

"It's nice to see you finally finding your way, but we can't send you out there. They won't let a teenager come back, no matter what you say."

"It's not like I'm a little kid." Marshal stood up. "Arthur pulled Excalibur from the stone when he was sixteen. I can deliver a simple message."

"I know you can," David said, motioning Marshal to sit down, "but I need you here. I have important things for you to do. You can't be spared." David turned to Liam. "Will Oliver go?"

"If I ask him."

"You know my words better than anyone." David slid down on the old leather couch with a sigh. "Tell him what to say and send him with my blessing."

Liam nodded, moving around his desk. "Lads, would you be kind enough to grab me a bullet-proof vest and a wee bit of something for a white flag?"

We stood as he walked past.

"I'll meet you at the front door."

I followed Marshal upstairs, blinking away the last echoes of nuclear destruction. His sudden participation in the church worried me. The shift left me feeling like someone had pulled the ground out from under my feet.

We grabbed duct tape, a white pillow case, and a broom handle from storage before heading to the gun room. The eerie calm of the deserted upstairs gave us the freedom to talk, but Marshal still whispered.

"Do you think he'll do it? Liam, I mean. Do you think he'll still drug David?"

"I don't know." I found it difficult to put my own confusion into words. I had no doubt David suffered from delusions, but the events of the past few hours made it difficult to ignore his visions. I had no idea how Liam would respond. "What do you think?"

"If you'd asked me an hour ago, I'd have said we were waiting too long to put him down."

"And now?"

"I don't know." Marshal grabbed a mostly complete vest, cursing under his breath for letting Rick take all the good ones to the gun show. "Everything he said he had a vision about is coming true."

"We don't know those blasts are going to spread the virus. He could still be wrong."

"Maybe." Marshal rarely looked as serious as he did now. "I guess we'll find out soon enough."

We headed back downstairs. Liam and Oliver waited for us by the front door. While Oliver slipped on the flak jacket, I duct-taped the white pillowcase to the broom handle.

"Crack the door, Marshal. Let's give the authorities a moment to see our white flag."

Marshal removed the boards that braced the door and opened it just a crack. Wincing, I extended the white flag. Even with my coat on, the frigid winter air sent shivers down my spine. A moment later, Oliver made Liam promise that he'd look after Karen and Maddie if anything happened to him. Marshal and I offered the same.

"Boys," Oliver said, as he took the pillowcase flag, "pray for me."

As I watched Oliver walk out the door with his arms raised high in the air, I couldn't help but think about the huge leap of faith that accompanied each and every step he took. When Rachel told me he was in on the plot to stop David, it was easy to imagine him as a doubting skeptic like me. As he crossed the bulldozed wasteland between the church and the FBI, I realized just how much faith he must have inside. I longed for that kind of certainty. It scared me how much I wanted it.

From the front door we could hear the government agents yell for him to drop to his knees and place his hands on his head. They left him there for almost ten minutes, kneeling in the frozen mud. Agents in body armor swarmed his position, dragging him off in cuffs. They led him out of view, leaving us to wait for their answer.

THE BEGINNING OF THE END

"LET'S GET ONE THING STRAIGHT. I NEVER THOUGHT A LOT OF you or your fat little friend," Liam said, "thumbing your nose at our rules, mocking the beliefs of everyone around you."

I looked past him to the closed telephone room door. After an hour and a half of waiting for Oliver, he told Marshal to keep watch and pulled me in for a little pep talk.

"But you've handled yourself like a man over this past week, so I'm going to treat you like one now. It's clear my Rachel's taken a shine to you. I just want to make sure we understand each other. Her 'reputation' is a fiction, dreamed up to get back at me for dragging her to Texas. She's not half the slapper she appears to be."

He didn't have to explain slapper to me. I knew exactly what he meant.

"I expect you to obey our rules, Cyrus. If you can do that and help me keep her safe, you'll win my approval. Do something to sully her name and I'll bury you right next to the shelter bus. Do we understand each other?"

I'd never heard Liam threaten anyone. The way he looked into my eyes without blinking sent a shiver down my spine. I nodded and then changed the subject. "What are you going to do about David? He's delusional ... but he's also right."

"I'm not sure if we should be more afraid of the FBI or these Fallen he keeps prattling on about." Liam took off his glasses and cleaned them on his white dress shirt. "What's your take on it?"

The idea that Liam would be asking my opinion about something that could save or kill everyone at Mount Carmel bothered me more than his threat to bury me if I touched Rachel. Part of me needed to believe that the adults were still in charge. That they knew what they were doing and I didn't have any responsibility to help fix this mess.

"I don't know," I said, looking back at the door. "I can't imagine the FBI's going to give us more time, not with mushroom clouds rising behind them. I'm sure they've got families to get out of harm's way. They're not going to be big on waiting. And the idea that they would seek refuge in this church. Come on."

"I agree. Unless Oliver comes back with good news, we drug David. There will be nothing left of us if the FBI mounts another assault, and I don't even want to imagine your president dropping more bombs."

Did we just decide that? I froze, scared to face the ramifications of a decision I didn't realize I was making. Liam reached into his front pocket and pulled out an oversized pen. Holding it in front of me, he unscrewed the top and produced two small plastic vials.

"All of the folders had a pen like this one. Should anything happen to me, mix it with any drink. According to the FBI, it's tasteless, odorless, and will only take a few minutes." Liam stowed one of the plastic vials in his suit jacket and put the other one back in the pen. He screwed on the top and handed it to me.

Before he could say anything else, Marshal knocked on the door and told us that Oliver was on his way back with an answer from the Feds. Liam and I traded glances. We could only hope for good news.

The first thing I noticed when Oliver walked through the door was they had confiscated his bulletproof vest. I guess that shouldn't have surprised me, but it did. In its place, he carried an oversized walkie-talkie.

"We have until noon tomorrow, and they were pretty ambivalent about giving us that long." Oliver handed Liam the portable two-way radio. "They're hoping the phone lines will be back up soon. This is just in case."

"And what happens if we don't surrender?" Marshal asked.

"Tanks and enough tear gas to put down a herd of elephants," Oliver replied. "They're prepared to drag us out, dead or alive. That's for sure."

"Tanks against civilians?" I couldn't bring myself to believe it. "They'd never get away with it."

"I don't know," Oliver said. "The President just declared martial law. Most of the press raced out of here after the blast. I'm surprised they're giving us until noon."

"We've got gas masks, don't we?" I asked.

"They only make them in adult sizes," Liam said, ushering us toward his office. "The little tykes would be defenseless."

The look on Marshal's face confirmed Liam's grim assessment. We were barely old enough to be fitted with an adult mask. That left forty kids and infants to endure the agony of chemical warfare. David's visions, true or not, no longer mattered. We had to do something to end this standoff before the FBI gassed the children.

David was sleeping on the leather couch, right were we left him. He opened his eyes as we settled in. "Bad news from the looks of you," he said to Oliver. "What's the word from the *Federales?*"

"They're giving us until noon tomorrow. It's surrender or tanks and tear gas for us."

"Things that bad for them?" David asked.

"They've got families, just like us, some not far from the border. Half of them have already deserted."

David sat up when he heard that news. I noticed a small spot of blood on his brown dress shirt. His bandages really needed changing. My mom usually doted on him. I wondered where she had gotten off to.

"According to the FBI, the majority of the people that get infected die. But the ones that don't, go mad. They turn crazy violent."

David was right again. I could only hope his streak ended when it came to the nuclear blast spreading the virus.

"What about the rest of the Feds," David asked, "the ones that stayed?"

"The straight arrows are still in charge ... but not by much."

"And the rest?"

"The rest are here for revenge. They haven't forgotten about the four agents we killed or the fifteen we wounded. They want payback."

Liam leaned against the front of his desk. "How did they respond to our offer?"

"They just about laughed me out of the room." Oliver put his hands in his pockets. "I don't know what to say about any of this. They promised to take us away from here, someplace safe from the radiation. They're all wearing exposure badges and Tyvek suits now. I guess it's horrible south of here."

Another problem we hadn't considered. If the movies I used to watch were remotely true, we'd have to deal with radiation fallout. I didn't know what made a tactical nuke different from a regular one or a movie one. Neither did anyone here, I suspected.

The FBI's loudspeakers started blaring again. The shrieking animal noises reminded us their patience was running thin. I looked at the overhead light. At least they left us with power this time.

"So what do we do?" Oliver asked. "They're not going to wait past tomorrow."

"God is waging a war against those who have rejected my message," David said. "As long as we stay here at Mount Carmel and remain true to His word, we will be saved."

"So God's going to destroy the world because the FBI attacked us?" I asked. "Do you have any idea how crazy that sounds? How unfair? There are five billion people out there, and most of them haven't the faintest clue about you or your message, much less the ATF and the FBI."

"The Third Seal," Marshal said, his eyes growing wide as David's biblical teachings took on real world consequences.

"The Third Seal," David repeated, his voice deflated. "You're right, Cyrus. It couldn't be more unfair. But you have to remember, the Bible told us centuries ago that the scales would be tipped, first against the world and then against us. From Revelation to Matthew to Hosea, the Merchant of the Third Seal charges a price that does not seem fair to the ways of man."

I looked over at Marshal. He nodded like he was buying the whole thing. I wanted to slap him out of it and make a run for my dad's place in West Virginia. The FBI didn't shoot Oliver. They wouldn't shoot us.

"Why don't you boys give us a moment alone," Liam said. "Cyrus, would you be kind enough to get David some dinner and a glass of that fresh milk."

"Save it for the kids," David said. "They need it more than I do."

"You have to eat something, David. You look terrible. Cyrus, be a good lad and scavenge him up dinner and something better than tap to drink."

"Sure," I said, trying not to linger on the point. "I'll find you an ice-cold beer."

David smirked and waved me out of the room. Marshal looked like he wanted to stay, but I pulled him into the hallway with me. Part of me worried that he might confess the entire plan. I could feel the pen Liam gave me in my back pocket. Should I try to hide it from Marshal?

We walked down to the kitchen and raided the cabinets. I opened up a can of beans and Marshal added half an MRE onto a plate, popping it into the microwave. While the meal heated up, I mixed a small pitcher of lemonade. The FBI said the drug was tasteless and odorless, but I didn't want to take any chances. I made it extra tart.

"Watch the door," I said.

"Why?"

That's when I produced the pen Liam had given me. Marshal's eyes went wide as he watched me unscrew the cap and pull out the small plastic vial.

"We have to ... for the kids." I twisted the tip of the vial until it came apart and then emptied the contents into the glass of lemonade. "It's not going to kill him."

Was I trying to convince Marshal or myself? Honestly, I didn't know. I grabbed a tray and loaded it up with food. When I turned for the door, Marshal was standing in my way. Would he stop me?

"There's no other way," I said.

Marshal stood there for what seemed like an eternity. While I didn't seem to understand the seriousness of my conversation with Liam in the phone room, Marshal knew full well how much rode on his choice.

"I hope you're right," he said, opening the door for me. "Because if you're not, we're all screwed."

PART SEVEN

They who dream by day
are cognizant of many things
which escape those
who dream only by night.
In their grey visions
they obtain glimpses
of eternity.

Edgar Allan Poe

THE THIRD SEAL

MARSHAL OPENED THE DOOR TO LIAM'S OFFICE FOR ME. I TOOK three steps in before noticing the gun in David's hand. I should have dropped the tray and made a run for it. Instead, I just froze.

"You can set the tray on Liam's desk," David said. "Marshal, close the door behind you."

Marshal must have missed the gun because he closed the door and then almost ran into me. I walked the tray over to Liam. He sat behind his desk, head hung low. I didn't know what had happened in the few minutes it took to microwave David's dinner, but everything had changed.

"Sit down, boys." There was a sharp edge to David's voice.

"What's going on?" Marshal asked.

"You boys were about to poison me." David waved the gun in Marshal's direction. "I think that's pretty clear."

"Why would we do that?" Marshal started to take a step in David's direction and then thought better of it, choosing instead to take a seat with me. "David, you're not thinking clearly. When was the last time Cyrus's mom changed your bandages?"

I had to hand it to Marshal. I knew his father had pointed guns at him and his mom when he was little, but I'd never seen anyone so calm with one in their face. I had to fight to keep from peeing my pants.

"You think I'm delusional? That's what you're going with, Marshal?"

"I just—"

"Do you think I didn't notice how Bud made sure you all had little blue folders? He's never been that organized in his life. The three of you have witnessed the fulfillment of prophecy. Did you think God would give me a vision of a plague sweeping away the nonbelievers and leave out your little plan to stop the salvation of everyone here?"

"The prophecy in Jerusalem." Liam cleared his throat, his voice shrinking with each word. "You called for Judgement Day three years from now. Isn't a wee bit of skepticism reasonable?"

"Is that what you call ganging up to poison me? Skepticism?" David waved his gun at the card table in the corner of Liam's office. Liam liked the super difficult puzzles, the three thousand piece ones with intentionally generic shapes.

"The vision God gave me is a little like those puzzles you love so much. At first you can barely wrap your brain around the idea that the pieces add up to anything. You can only find the corners, the edge of the thing. And as far as the center goes, you put the wrong pieces together, or you're just looking at them the wrong way.

"Some pieces seem years off when they're sooner than you think, or they belong to a different part of the puzzle, a different place and time. The more the pieces come together, the clearer the picture becomes. And when you get down to the last, precious few, you know exactly where they go. That's why my visions were years off, Liam. And that's why they're spot on, as you like to say, now that the Seals are finally breaking."

David shifted on the couch, wincing in pain. "I'm disappointed in you, Cyrus. I didn't expect it would be you betraying me. I suppose in the grand scheme of things, that makes sense. I just hoped—you and I shared so much."

"I'm sorry," I said, staring at the gun. I couldn't muster the courage to play it cool like Marshal. "I just didn't want people to— I didn't want to get hurt."

David nodded. I could see disappointment and understanding in his eyes.

"The children—" Liam started.

"Will be saved by God. They won't choke to death on the FBI's tear gas. I can promise you that much."

"What are you going to do with us?" Marshal asked.

"Well, I'm not going to shoot you if that's what you're worried about. God needs you, all three of you. I just can't have you serving me up on a platter. Understand?"

"Not really," I replied.

"Son, I'm not stalling the FBI for the reasons you think. I'm not afraid of their judgment. We got no drugs here. No giant stockpile of illegal weapons. I'm trying to keep you alive."

I'm sure he mistook the look on my face for disbelief. In truth, him calling me son pissed me off more than anything he had to say. "What about the girls? A judge isn't going to care if their parents consented. And it's going to be hard not to notice how many you've married, not to mention the kids."

"I'm right with God's law. Soon, the rest won't matter. All the tanks and tear gas in the world won't be worth a hill of beans when the Fallen swallow them whole. The FBI won't make it to noon."

"And what if you're wrong?" Liam asked.

"I tell you what. They gave me till noon tomorrow. I'll march everyone out of here an hour before if they're still asking." David waved the gun in Liam's direction. "That fair enough to satisfy you?"

Liam nodded, never taking his focus off the gun.

"Good. Now the rest of our church needs to be reinforced like the front door. I want boards shoring up every opening, even upstairs. Pull them out of the walls if you have to, but see to it. It's the most important thing you've ever done. Take Marshal with you."

"What about me?" I asked.

"You and me. We've got unfinished business."

David cocked the gun and pointed Marshal and Liam to the door. As soon as they closed it behind them, he told me to wedge a chair under the doorknob. It's not as easy as it looks in the movies. I tried two different chairs and neither worked very well. Short of dragging a bookcase in front of the door, I didn't see an easy answer.

"So which did you poison?" David asked. "The food or the drink?"

"How do you know I didn't poison both?" I said, frustrated with the door.

"I hope not. I'm starving." He set the gun next to him on the couch. "Stop fiddling with the chairs. Wedge the coatrack against the door. I just want a few seconds warning if Liam comes back armed."

"Do you think he'd do that?"

"He just tried to get you to poison me."

"It's not poison," I said, taking a seat across from David. "It's just some stuff that's supposed to knock you out."

"And you trust the FBI enough to say you know that for sure?"

I only had Liam and Rachel's word. And they were relying on the FBI's. Given the government's actions here, David had a good point.

"Seriously, did you poison the food?"

"No," I said, looking at the lemonade with a newfound suspicion the FBI set us all up, "just the drink."

"Then would you mind grabbing the tray for me?"

I left the spiked lemonade on Liam's desk and handed David the tray of food. For an instant, his hands were occupied and my eyes drifted over the gun at his side. I could grab it before he could stop me, but what would I do with it? Shoot him? Force him to drink lemonade that might kill him? I wasn't sure enough that he was wrong to risk it. Our eyes met when I looked up from the gun.

It felt like a test. Turning back to my chair, I could only hope I passed. Without the gun, I needed his trust.

"I'm not going to miss this food, I can tell you that much." David grimaced at the taste of military rations. "The apocalypse almost sounds good after a few days of this crap."

"How close are we?"

David paused with his mouth full of reconstituted omelet. At this point, everybody knew the beef rations tasted a hundred times better, but he saved those for the wives and kids. The omelets coated your teeth with a sour, pasty gunk that the adults joked could outlast any FBI siege. He swallowed hard, stopping short of his next bite.

"We're close." After a few more bites, he stifled a belch and sat the plate aside. "How are things with Rachel? I couldn't help but notice your arm around her during the President's speech. I hope Liam's not giving you too hard a time?"

"He's not happy about it."

"Fathers rarely are. I had the same problem when I was your age. Of course, I wasn't half as cool as you like to pretend to be. Met a girl that I thought was the love of my life. Everything inside me said this is the one, like God had decided it for me."

"What happened?"

"Her parents weren't having any of it." He scanned the wood-paneled walls like he was looking back to a different life. "I proposed when she got pregnant, and they threw me out of their house. I set out to be the best father, the best man I could, but they forced her to get an abortion. Said she wasn't going to ruin her life over the likes of me."

"That sounds awful," I said.

"I just wanted a simple life. A wife. A family. Maybe a little time on the weekends to play guitar. It wasn't in the cards. God had other plans for me." He took a deep breath and gave the omelet a second look. "I'd offer to help you smooth things over with Liam, but it's going to take a lot more than a good word from me to get him to come around. Right now, I suspect he's just praying I know what I'm talking about. He can sense the end is near. He just needs something to remind him why he came all the way to Waco."

David forced himself to take another bite. "Do you remember when I told you the world doesn't end with the apocalypse?"

"It just changes, you said."

"Right. The end is just the beginning. After we're gone, it will be up to you to decide what kind of world this becomes. Don't worry. This is part of God's plan for you. I know you don't believe that, but some things are true whether you believe in them or not. After the end, you'll run into other folks like me. People who see the truth that escapes those who only dream at night. Protect them. They're humanity's last hope. That's your charge from God. Understand?"

"Not even a little."

"One day you'll find the courage to believe, and when you do, all of this will make sense to you. I promise."

"And what happens to the Davidians, the true believers? Are you transported to Jerusalem for the final battle?"

"I don't know."

It had been a while since I heard those words out of David's mouth. Had he been steering all these people to a destination even he couldn't see?

"You've got to remember, God gave me a vision and a purpose, not the ability to look into the future at will. I know our destination, but God hasn't revealed everything to me. He's shown me enough of the road ahead to trust in His plan. To trust in you."

"I don't want anything to do with God's plan. I just want to do my own thing."

"So did I, Cyrus." He took off his glasses. "But like the song says, you can't always get what you want."

His eyes seemed so old to me, so weighed down by the burden of a life chosen for him. Real or imagined, he carried the fate of the world on his shoulders. For the first time, I felt like I understood David, and that scared the crap out of me.

Something crashed against the outside of the church, just above us. I flinched as a second and third impact slammed into the upstairs, followed by half a dozen more. Were they launching rockets at us now? I dropped to the floor, tensing for explosions that didn't come.

"Sounds like the FBI just realized the Fallen are rising up all around them." David reached for the gas mask on the edge of Liam's desk. The simple effort of leaning forward seemed almost too much for him. "It's time."

"Tear gas?" I looked to the door and then back at David. "But you said—"

"I said the children wouldn't choke to death. I didn't say the FBI wouldn't give it their best shot."

I could hear more canisters being launched at the building. It sounded like they were bouncing off the doors we had nailed over the windows. I heard the sound of wood splintering upstairs.

"What do we do?"

"There's nothing we can do. We just have to ride it out. It's time to trust in God's plan, Cyrus."

He handed me the gas mask.

"What about you?"

"I don't think I can stand on my own, much less make it to the vault. You're going to have to lug my sorry ass."

FOG OF WAR

THE THING NOBODY TELLS YOU ABOUT GAS MASKS IS THEY MAKE it almost impossible to breathe. Under the best of situations, it feels like somebody's trying to smother you with a pillow. You can't catch your breath or shake the claustrophobic feeling that there's some kind of weird creature camped on your face. Or in my case, a vicious little monster biting the hell out of my injured ear.

Just getting David up and out the door had me gasping for air. Outside Liam's office, thin wisps of smoke trailed down the top of the front stairs. By comparison, the main floor seemed clear of gas. From the sound of David's cough, I knew that wasn't the case.

"Hold tight," I said. The mask mangled my words, but David gripped my shoulder hard enough for me to drag him down the long hall.

The lenses in my mask fogged up long before I made it to the kitchen. This wasn't like carrying David downstairs to meet the sheriff. He didn't have any strength left in him to help me. At some point, I turned on instinct and clipped a doorway, almost dropping his dead weight. Gas canisters crashed into boarded-up windows all around us. Thankfully, I didn't hear any on the first floor give way.

I could feel my left hand brush against the plastic shower curtains, which meant I was in the right place. David got heavier with each step. I had to get him into the vault before I passed out. I stumbled through a slit in the curtains. If Oliver hadn't grabbed me, I would have walked head first into the closed vault door.

"You can't go in there without exposing the children!" He reached out with his hands. "I can take David for you!"

I saw Mom in the corner behind Oliver, trying to treat second-degree chemical burns with damp towels, gauze, and a dwindling supply of what I assumed to be some kind of chemical neutralizer. Oliver sat David down next to her while I tried to catch my breath.

"Have you seen Rachel?" I yelled. "Or Marshal?"

"Last time I saw Marshal, he was upstairs near David's room. I don't know about Rachel."

Just then Rodney body-slammed me in a manic dash for the vault door. It took all three of us to keep him from opening it. Rodney had chemical burns on his face and it looked like he had tried to claw his own eyes out. I thought he was going to take Oliver's head off, but the cagey Armenian dropped him with one punch.

I caught Rodney on his way down and helped Oliver carry him to Mom's makeshift trauma ward.

"David's room?" I repeated. "You sure?"

Oliver just shrugged.

I patted him on the shoulder and pointed upstairs, ducking under the shower curtains. I could hear Mom yelling for me to come back, but I wasn't about to leave my best friends to claw their eyes out. I had to save them.

I cut through the cafeteria and bounded up the back steps. Without David's weight, it felt like I could fly. I screeched to a halt when I got to the women's dorm. The tear gas that only appeared in thin wisps downstairs blanketed the long hallway with a cloud of poison. I couldn't see the patchwork of doors nailed over grenade holes in the floor.

I moved from room to room, secretly thanking God for Liam's decision to relocate the women and children to the vault. Without an air supply, they couldn't stay in there forever, but I didn't want to imagine what would have happened if they had stayed upstairs. Like Liam said, nobody makes gas masks for children.

The tear gas grew thicker as I made my way down the long hall. None of the windows on this end of the building had been breached. I couldn't help but stop at the top of the front steps. Gas obscured the bloodstains from the ATF agent that shot me, but I knew they were still there. If David hadn't dove on me, I'd be missing more than just a chunk of my ear.

I turned left and headed for David's room. I could tell the tear gas had breached his window and the gun room. Smoke billowed out of both doors. I couldn't see three feet in front of me. I hadn't heard any gunshots over the screeching loudspeakers, but I couldn't shake the fear that FBI agents would be waiting for me in the poisonous mist.

"Marshal! Can you hear me? Rachel!"

Nothing.

I couldn't see past my own elbow in David's room. Even the busted-out window didn't provide any relief. I crouched, but the air barely cleared. There were dozens of tear gas canisters on the floor. They looked like Campbell's Soup cans with nubby little fins. I tried to pick one up and throw it out the window, but the thing burned my hand the moment I touched it.

Just about the time I confirmed no one was in the room, a tear gas canister sailed past my head and slammed into the wall behind me. I dropped to the floor. I could hear more canisters hitting boarded up windows along the back of the building. How much gas was the FBI going to fire into our church?

"Marshal! Rachel! Anybody?"

I crawled across the hall to the gun room, kicking live canisters out of my way. There was a Marshal-shaped body near the front window. I raced to him.

A tear gas canister had shattered the corner of his mask. The side of his head was covered in blood. His eyes were swelled shut and his mask was half full of vomit. I couldn't tell if he was still breathing.

"Marshal!" I screamed, pulling him back from the window. I had to stand up to drag him away. He was a lot heavier than David. I pulled him by his coat, a couple feet at a time. In the middle of the room, I slipped on a tear gas canister and dropped to the floor, cracking the left lens on my mask.

It didn't shatter.

I pulled myself up and started dragging Marshal toward the door. I could feel my eyes tearing up, a sure sign some of the gas was getting through. I had to fight to keep them open. They burned worse with every step.

My eyes and nose started running like open faucets. I couldn't make out the shape of the room. It was getting hard to breathe through my nose and I couldn't stifle the coughing fits that came with the burning in my throat. I tried to hold my breath until I could get Marshal into the hall. The air had to be better out there.

I got him halfway down the hallway and slipped on the chemical-soaked floor. I couldn't see. I couldn't breathe. I wasn't going to make it downstairs, with or without Marshal. I wanted to claw my eyes out to stop the pain, but I couldn't manage to get the mask off.

Just then I felt strong arms grab me from behind and pull me down the hallway. We didn't go far. I remember the uneven floor cutting into my back and the sound of a door opening. My face felt like it was melting. I never imagined pain like this.

"Stop screaming!" a voice said through the muffle of a gas mask. Someone stepped over me and I heard a mad dash of footsteps in the hallway. I fumbled with my mask, but it wouldn't come off. The footsteps returned and I felt something being dragged past me.

I started to scream when the mask was ripped from my face, but a deluge of water drowned out my cries. I reached out with my hands to stop it, but someone batted them away. I wanted to die.

Someone pulled a different mask over my face, this one much tighter, and told me again to stop screaming. My face no longer burned, though my eyes and throat were still on fire. I couldn't stop coughing, but I could breathe.

I could breathe!

I forced my eyes open long enough to recognize the storage room. The new mask wasn't cracked, but tears still poured out of my eyes and nose. I was lying in a pool of water. I closed my eyes tight and tried to sit up. The room felt like it was tilting in on me.

When I forced my eyes open again, I could see someone pouring a bucket of mop water over Marshal's head. I couldn't make out the masked face, but I recognized the hair.

"Rachel?" She ripped off Marshal's shattered gas mask and replaced it with a fresh one. "How?"

She bounded over me with a roll of duct tape in her hand. I blinked hard as she added a layer to the door seams. When she came back to check on me, I looked deep into her eyes. They held none of the panic that I saw on Oliver's and my mom's faces. She had a strong-willed look of determination that gave me hope I could get out of this alive.

"You okay?" she asked. "I didn't think you were ever going to stop screaming."

It felt like someone had poured acid in my eyes and down my throat, but I could see and breathe. I blinked hard again, my eyes still thin slits. The three of us were in a cramped, windowless storage closet. I realized she must have dragged us both here and used the mop water to flush the chemicals from our eyes and faces. My body shuddered at the thought of dingy mop water, but it was pure genius.

"How did you—" I stopped myself, looking past Rachel to Marshal. He wasn't moving. I rushed to his side.

"He's breathing," she said. "I don't know if he'll be okay, but he's alive."

He had chemical burns on the right side of his face. I turned and hugged her as hard as I could.

"I don't know how you did it, but I love you."

The distant echo of gunfire interrupted our embrace. My first thought was the FBI, but it sounded far away. Marshal mumbled something, and we both leaned closer to him. He didn't open his eyes, but he licked his lips and tried to take a deep breath.

"Too far," he finally said, the words choked off by a shallow coughing fit. If it wasn't coming from the FBI, where was it coming from? The intensity of the gunfire increased, and the sound of a series of distant explosions punctuated the fighting. "Getting closer," he added.

The gas canisters stopped slamming into the side of the church. Rachel gave me an ominous glare.

"Go," Marshal insisted. "Find out."

"Find out what?" I asked.

"The Third Seal."

Rachel and I hesitated, both scared he wasn't delusional.

"Go." Marshal rolled to his side and managed to pull himself up against the back of the closet wall. "We need answers."

PART EIGHT

We wrap up our violent and mysterious world
in a pretense of understanding.
We paper over the voids of our comprehension
with science and religion,
and make believe that order has been imposed.

Until that moment
when something from the cold unknown
reaches up to take us.

Mark Lawrence

A BEACON IN THE DARKNESS

Rachel helped me up, and we were out the door before I could protest. Without the constant assault of tear gas canisters, the hallway mist had already cleared a bit, but we still couldn't see the floor. We made our way down the long hall, careful not to trip and fall. The chemicals from the tear gas stained the white walls a faded red.

Halfway down the hallway, we made it to the barricaded door that led to the residential tower. My gas-addled brain struggled to wrap itself around David's vision. His predictions had gone from mystic mumbo-jumbo to educated guesses to what, on the other side of that door, might become startling fact.

"Do you think David's crazy?" Rachel asked.

"I don't know anymore."

We unblocked the door and made our way up the dark stairway. Thick blankets covered the third floor windows, which were somehow still intact. I fumbled in the dark for the binoculars hanging off the telescope and edged close to the windows for a peek.

Between the gas mask and the FBI's bright floodlights, I couldn't see a lot. My eyes slowly adjusted, and it became clear that

Waco was burning in the distance. Nearer to our standoff, tiny flashes of semi-automatic gunfire lit up the darkness. From the look of it, the gunfire was retreating our way.

Rachel joined me at the window. The Seven Seals. The Fallen. Could the whole thing be true?

Even without binoculars, Rachel could see the gunfire light up the night like fireflies. "Maybe he's not so crazy after all ..."

"Or maybe he's crazy and he's right."

The once bright perimeter, where the FBI had moved the press for their own protection, was now shrouded in darkness. From the looks of the thinning patterns of gunfire, the retreating agents were being overrun.

"What are we going to do?" Rachel asked. "It looks like they're headed directly for us."

I didn't have an answer for her. Whatever had burned Waco was headed our way with impossible speed. The flashes of gunfire trailed off, disappearing just short of the FBI siege.

When I got my first glimpse of the Fallen, it shocked me. I don't know if I expected demons or monsters or what, but these looked like ordinary teenagers. They rushed the FBI camp like it was the playing field of a championship football game.

The FBI must have had some idea of what was coming because they opened fire as soon as the teens entered the camp. I've never seen anything like it. FBI agents shooting kids. I kept waiting for their gunfire to repel the onslaught, but the teens took shot after shot and just kept coming. When one finally did fall, three more seemed to leap out of the darkness to take their place. Were they really under the control of Lucifer? Watching these impossibly fast creatures race headlong into gunfire, I had to wonder.

I gasped as an older kid, one that looked like a blood-soaked model for Abercrombie and Fitch, ripped an agent's arm clean out of its socket. A girl in a pizza delivery uniform dove past him, tackling another agent. A gunshot wound to her chest didn't stop her from clawing his face off.

Rachel couldn't see the gruesome detail without the binoculars, but she could hear the shrieks of the agents, even over the FBI's loudspeakers. They called out for God to save them. I guess God had stopped listening. The Fallen teens gouged out eyes, ripped off scalps, ate ears. It was like nothing I had ever seen. They didn't touch the guns. They seemed hell-bent on doing all their damage by hand. I watched them drag half-dismembered bodies around like trophies.

Rachel took a step toward the telescope, but I grabbed her arm, stopping her. "You don't want to see this," I said.

She pulled away, stepping past me to take a look. Some things you have to see with your own eyes.

It took the Fallen almost no time to overwhelm the rest of the camp. And when they did, Rachael and I noticed a sudden shift in their collective focus. They didn't turn their attention our way, thank God. As a matter of fact, it was almost like we were invisible to them. Instead, they set about the destruction of the floodlights and giant loudspeakers blaring at us.

One thought struck me like a thunderbolt.

"We've got to kill the power! Once they knock out the FBI's lights, they'll notice ours." I dropped the binoculars, grabbed Rachel's hand, and rushed down the steps. I fell down the last three or four, stumbling out the second floor entrance and slamming into Liam. His gas mask looked more than a little out of place with his suit.

"What the blazes is going on?" he asked. "That door should be secured!"

"The Fallen are here," Rachel said. "They're really here!"

"What are you talking about?"

"They've overrun the FBI," I replied. "The floodlights and loudspeakers are driving them crazy."

Liam looked up at the second floor's fluorescent overhead lights. I could see the same thought occur to him, only he didn't waste any more time talking. He made a run for the front stairs.

We followed, bounding down the steps in a mad dash for the chapel. Three church members sat in the pews, their gas masks bowed in silent prayer, the surreal moment punctuated by the FBI's bright lights illuminating the uncovered tops of the tall stained glass windows. Liam rushed up the stage and into a little utility room, tucked just to the side of the gym's double doors.

The main circuit breaker had a long-arm kill switch with a lock on it. Liam fumbled for the right key among the dozens he kept on the ring attached to his belt. Rachel pushed past him before he could find the right one, pulling open the breaker box and switching individual circuits off as quickly as she could.

Sections of the church powered down. Liam dropped his keys and joined her, slamming the individual circuits on his side of the box off. The utility room went dark.

Two seconds later, the FBI's loudspeakers went silent.

We all stood there in the dark, scared to even breathe. The winter winds of Texas carried the unamplified shrieks of the Fallen as they reveled in their victory.

"How bad is it?" Liam asked.

"David was right. The FBI never had a chance." Rachel tightened her grip on my hand. "Cyrus, what are we going to do?"

I didn't know where to start. The victorious cries of the Fallen faded and an eerie calm settled over the church.

"We need to get Marshal to my mom," I said. "And we need to talk to David, see if he has any idea what's happening next. But first, we need to secure the door to the tower. If those things get in here, we're all done for."

"I don't suppose anyone brought a flashlight?" Rachel asked.

THE WAITING GAME

UNDER NORMAL CIRCUMSTANCES, IT TAKES TEAR GAS THIRTY minutes to dissipate. At least, that's what my mom told me. Fired into an enclosed space like our church, with all the windows and doors boarded up, nobody knew how long it would last.

It's like the vault Mom ordered shut at the start of the gas attack. There's no ventilation system inside that thing. No way of knowing how long the women and children can last without fresh air. At least not without a bunch of math you can't do in a gas mask in the middle of the apocalypse.

You just have to push it as long as you think you can. You don't want babies choking on poison, but you don't want them suffocating either. An hour after the attack, my mom took off her mask and tested the air.

The remnant swirl of chemicals floating in the cafeteria brought tears to her eyes and gave her a momentary coughing fit, but she could breathe without toppling over, and that was a much better fate than dying in the vault.

Much to everyone's surprise, the upstairs fared better. Once the gas canisters stopped spewing their deadly mist, the holes they had torn in the upstairs windows helped to ventilate the entire floor. I wouldn't call the air fresh, but you could breathe it without a mask.

Rachel and I split up. She got Marshal downstairs, where Mom could tend to the burns on his face, while I helped the men secure the tower and barricade the doors to the breached rooms. It might have made more sense to seal the windows, but word of the Fallen spread like wildfire, and the guys were petrified of attracting Lucifer's attention. God helps those who help themselves, they reminded me.

With their masks off, the grownups all had the same blank stare. They looked like bombed out war refugees, unable to focus on anything but the moment in front of them. That wasn't me. I had seen the Fallen firsthand. I wanted answers. I wanted to know what was going to happen next.

When the guys started work on the last door, I snuck away. Without a flashlight, the darkness turned the upstairs into a mine-field. I couldn't even lean on the walls as a guide. Whole sections had been pulled apart to reinforce the doors. Halfway down the long hall, I tripped on a door that someone had nailed to the floor and went down hard on my shoulder. Thankfully, Rachel showed up at the top of the front steps with a lantern and led me down to Liam's office.

Marshal was sprawled out on the couch with a thick layer of gauze duct taped to the right side of his face. High-tech medicine at its best. David had moved to the fold-out table. He had a Maglite pointed down at Liam's puzzle and was noodling with the edges of it. Next to the puzzle, his gun and the walkie-talkie the FBI had given Oliver.

"Can anyone hear me?" From the sound of the distant voice, it wasn't the first time he'd asked. "For the love of God, just answer. I need help. I'm begging you! They're everywhere!"

It sounded like the sheriff's voice, minus the calm. We could hear the all too human screeches of the Fallen in the background. The savage teens relentlessly pounded on the outside of what I guessed to be the negotiating team's mobile command center. Their frustrated wails sent a chill down my spine.

"David, please. Just talk to me. Tell me what you want. I've got Rick Marsh here with me. He wants to come home."

"Skywalker's uncle?" I said.

"The lad's name's Cameron," Liam corrected as he came into the room behind me. "Not *Skywalker*."

I started to say something I'd regret, but the walkie-talkie interrupted me.

"David, this is Rick. I sure hope you're all doing okay in there. Listen, I just wanted you to know that I cleared up the whole gun thing with the FBI. They understand it was all for the shows. Took a while to get all the permits together, but the sheriff backed me up, and they're ready to drop those charges. At least they were. I don't suppose it matters much now. They sent me here to talk you out, but I guess you're probably safer in there. I don't know, man, it's pretty bad out here. David? You are there, aren't ya? Come on, man, give us some hope."

David placed another puzzle piece and started rooting around for the next one. Marshal looked at me and then the gun. Nobody spoke.

"Fine," Rachel said, crossing the room in a huff. She reached past David's gun and snatched the walkie-talkie. He didn't stop her.

"Mr. Marsh, this is Rachel—Liam's daughter. We hear you."

"Rachel! Sweet Rachel. Thank God! We thought your radio died or you shut it off or worse. We're trapped out here."

"Where are you?" Rachel asked.

"In the hostage—in the negotiating truck. They turned it over, but they haven't managed to get in. I don't suppose there's any way you could see fit to come out here and get us?"

"I'm not sure how we'd do that." Rachel looked around the room for ideas. Nobody had one. "Do you have any food or water? Maybe you can wait them out."

"Stale takeout and a couple sodas, not enough to last very

long." You could hear the Fallen shaking the vehicle. "They seem hell-bent on getting in here."

I motioned for the radio.

"This is Cyrus. Can I talk to Sheriff Reynolds?"

"Go ahead."

"Sheriff, if you have anything that lights up or makes noise inside there, you might want to shut it down. I got a pretty good look at things from the tower here. As soon as they took out the agents shooting at them, they ripped the lights and speakers apart. I could be wrong, but it seemed like the lights and sounds were driving them crazy."

"That's not a bad idea," the sheriff said. "You think they might lose interest?"

I looked David's way. He shook his head.

"Maybe," I said. "Either way, you need to sit tight and conserve the radio while we try to figure something out. Anything you can tell us from your end?"

"We're pretty blind out here. No windows in the mobile command center, but I did get a good look outside before things went south."

"What did you see?"

"It's kinda hard to explain. They told us they'd all be kids, but—"

He stopped, and we could hear the sound of the Fallen stripping away metal from the outside of the vehicle. None of us knew how much time they had left.

"I got a good look at them upstairs, through a pair of binoculars. You still with me?"

"I started out as a beat cop in San Antonio," Sheriff Reynolds continued. "My rookie year, I ran into this kid, maybe seventeen years old. He was stoned out of his mind on PCP. Skinny little bastard put his fist through a squad-car window and just about choked the life out of my partner. It's like an army of junkies out here. Whatever they're hopped up on, it's scrambled their minds and supercharged their bodies."

"Thanks for that," I said.

The sound of metal being pulled off their vehicle stopped and was replaced by a chorus of frustrated screeches.

"We've gone dark here," I said. "I think you should do the same. Maybe we could check back with each other in an hour. See if we can come up with a plan or something."

"Thank you," he said. "Keep safe."

"Cyrus, this is Rick again. Please make sure Cameron's okay. Tell him I love him."

"You can tell him yourself when you check back." I looked at the clock sitting on Liam's desk. "It's ten till nine. We'll turn the radio back on at ten."

I turned the radio off and put it back on the table, not knowing if I would ever hear from either of them again. David continued fiddling with the puzzle. Marshal was sitting up now, but he still looked like he was in bad shape. Liam just stood there.

The idea of rescuing them just reeked of stupidity. Still, my mind couldn't help but come back to the question of how to pull it off. Looking at Rachel, I could see the same question weighing on her.

"We can't help them, Cyrus," David said. "No matter how much we might want to. Their chance at redemption has passed."

Wasn't seeing the future enough for David? He had to add mind reading? I heard someone out in the hall yell that the last of the FBI spotlights had just come crashing down. Liam turned for the door and muttered something about getting everyone ready.

"I was just thinking," I said before Liam could make it out of the room, "about how much the speakers and lights bothered them. Marshal and I have a pretty serious stockpile of fireworks. We could—"

"Distract them?" The sarcasm practically dripped from Liam's mouth. "Your heart's in the right place, Cyrus, but this isn't one of your American action movies. From what you said the Fallen did to the FBI, mounting a rescue would only get us all damned to Hell."

"You don't know that." I turned to David. He had one eye cocked my way. "You told me I'd end up choosing the type of world that came next. If that's true, it's not going to be the kind where I walk away from someone begging me for help. Not when I can do something about it."

"That's a ways down the road for you, son." David turned a puzzle piece over and over in his hand and then offered me a pained smile. "Right now, it's my job to make sure you live long enough to see it."

PART NINE

Belief may be no more, in the end,
than a source of energy,
like a battery which one clips
into an idea to make it run ...
Believing whatever has to be believed
in order to get the job done.

J.M. Coetzee

SKYWALKER

WITHOUT POWER, WE WERE ONCE AGAIN AT THE MERCY OF THE frigid winds of the Texas plains. The temperature inside the church dropped dramatically, and this time we all knew it wasn't coming back up. Oliver brought David's kerosene heater down to Liam's office. I stayed there for a while, holding Rachel under her father's ever-vigilant gaze, but somebody had to break the news to Skywalker before the next check in. I guess I decided that somebody was me.

I found him in the vault ferrying fresh water to the new moms. The air in the cafeteria had improved, but not fast enough for the babies. Their late night cries echoed in the concrete vault, creating an angry symphony of protest against the government that had attacked us. Skywalker handed Oliver's wife a fresh bucket of water and grabbed two empties from the corner. I stood in the doorway, blocking his exit.

"You mind getting out of my way? Some of us have actual work to do."

"Cameron, we need to talk."

He dropped the empty buckets. I never called him Cameron.

"What's going on?"

"It's your uncle. He's—well, he's trapped in a van outside. He got through to us on the radio."

"Is he okay?"

I tried to give Skywalker the look. You know, the one that says this isn't the kind of conversation you have in front of small children and their worried mothers, but I could tell his feet were rooted to the spot, his jaw clenched in anticipation of horrible news.

"Your uncle's trapped like us—but he's safe." I decided to leave out the part about the claustrophobic van and the raging monster teens. He'd find out about that soon enough. "He's with the sheriff. David's getting ready to talk to both of them again. I thought you might like to be in on the conversation."

Skywalker looked me up and down, trying to decide if this was the meanest prank I'd ever pulled. I bent down and grabbed the buckets for him. Something else I never do.

"Why don't we drop these off and go talk to your uncle? Someone else can help with the water."

"Yeah," he finally mustered in a faraway voice. "Thanks."

By the time I got him back to Liam's office, I could hear Sheriff Reynold's muffled voice on the walkie-talkie. I opened the door and put my arm on Skywalker's shoulder, easing him into the room. You could still hear the Fallen screeching in the background, but they no longer sounded like they were trying to claw their way into the mobile command center.

"—at least until they run out of other things to tear apart," Sheriff Reynolds said. "Shutting everything down was a good idea. You'll have to thank Cyrus for me."

"You can thank him yourself," David said. "He just brought Cameron in to talk to Rick."

I nudged Skywalker toward the walkie-talkie. He hesitated, crossing the room in fits and starts. The Fallen howled in the background, filling the lull with their otherworldly cries.

"You okay?" Skywalker finally asked.

"Don't worry about me," Rick said. "I've been in tougher scrapes than this. How you holding up?"

"You don't have to worry. We're protected in here. How close are you?"

Something large and metal crashed to the ground, maybe one of the portable light poles. Skywalker jumped at the sound.

"We're in the main camp. If we had a window in the back of this truck, I could see you from here. Then again, if we had a window, we'd be dead."

"Maybe they'll forget about you." Skywalker looked to David and Liam and then me. "We could sneak them in. They'd be safe with us."

"It's too late for that," David said. "Our doors are closed to the outside world."

I started to say something, but Rick cut me off.

"Listen to me, boy. I need you to be strong. The sheriff and I talked it through. We can't take the chance that we'd lead these monsters back to you. There are too many innocent women and children in there. I need you to stay inside and help protect them."

Tears streamed down Skywalker's face.

"We're safe right now, and we're going to find a way out of this spot. You hear me?"

"Yes, sir."

His voice sounded so small. Rachel got up from the couch and put her arms around him. Even I wanted to give Skywalker a big hug, but there was nothing I could do or say to make this better.

"Have you heard from Mom?" he asked.

Rick started to answer and then stopped himself. I didn't know a lot about Skywalker's mom, other than the fact that she was a roadie for some endlessly touring tribute band. She never came to Mount Carmel or called him. Skywalker kept a picture of her in an old pocket watch that didn't work, carried that thing everywhere. I'm ashamed to say I'd teased him about it on more than one occasion.

"Now you know I haven't heard a peep out of her in over three years."

"I just thought maybe, with us being on TV and stuff, she'd see us and call."

"It's just me and you, partner, and I need you to hold up your end of the fort for a while. At least until I can figure a way out of this mess. I want you to do what David and Liam tell you to do. They're the closest thing you got to family right now. You hear me?"

"Okay."

"We should probably sign off," Rick said. "Neither of us knows how long these batteries are going to hold out. We'll lie low and check back at the top of the hour. Cameron, I love you. Don't forget that."

"I love you, too."

We heard from them again at eleven and twelve, but they missed their one a.m. check-in and we could barely hear them at two. After that, nothing. I suppose I should have tried to get some sleep, but I just couldn't get Rick and the sheriff off my mind. They were out there alone with no one left to protect them.

Skywalker couldn't sleep either. I told him the lack of communication amounted to a dead radio on their end of things. No news didn't have to be bad news. I even took him upstairs to the tower, but with the floodlights gone, we couldn't see anything through the telescope or binoculars.

So we just sat up there in the wee hours, waiting for the dawn to bring us answers.

"You ever wonder where your dad is?" Skywalker asked.

"Sometimes. Not as much as I used to." I reached down to retie my boots. "He's somewhere in West Virginia with his new family."

I knew exactly where he was.

"I heard he left after your brother died."

I shot Skywalker an angry glare. I don't know why. It's not like he was making fun of me. And with his mom on the road with a drugged-up freak show, he didn't have any room to talk about my family.

"I was just wondering if my mom was still out there and thought you might be thinking the same about your dad."

The sound of the Fallen tearing apart God knows what punctuated the long silence between us. I needed rest, but I knew I wouldn't sleep.

"Mom crawled into a bottle of vodka when my brother died. After about a year of trying to save her, Dad crawled into bed with the nanny. That was about five years ago. I haven't seen much of him since. We aren't exactly close."

"What happened? To your brother, I mean."

I started to put him off. I didn't like talking about Michael, not even to Marshal or Rachel. But the look in Skywalker's eyes said he needed something, anything, to distract him from the fact that his uncle would soon be dead—if he wasn't already.

"Mom and Dad rented this beach house in North Carolina the summer I turned nine, and they let Michael bring his high school girlfriend, Kelly. She was the kind of girl that nine-year-old boys dream about stealing from their older brothers. Smart. Flirty. I don't think she had any idea how pretty she was to me."

"I've never been to the ocean," Skywalker said.

"I've never been back." I shifted my left leg to keep it from falling asleep. "We were both scared of the water, Michael and me. I'd been stung by jellyfish the summer before, and he'd seen *Jaws*."

Skywalker gave me a questioning look.

"It's a movie about a giant shark that eats people," I said. "Anyway, we were both keen to impress Kelly and dared each other to go farther and farther out until the riptide grabbed us both."

"You must have been scared."

"Dad pulled me out of the water before I even realized I could've died. He sent me back to the house with Kelly for help and went after Michael. The Coast Guard had to pull Dad out of the water before he drowned himself searching. All I could do was stand by the shore like an idiot and wait to find out if I still had an older brother. The Coast Guard never found his body."

"I'm so sorry. That's horrible."

"Thing is, Dad didn't hesitate or look for someone else to act. He went after us like his whole life depended on it. He's a bastard for what he did to Mom, but when I think about how he went after Michael without any thought for his own life, I wish I could be more like him."

"Seems like you are to me," Skywalker said.

"If I was, your uncle and the sheriff wouldn't be sitting out there alone."

"It's not the same thing, and you know it. I'm sure you'll make your father proud when the time comes. Most kids wouldn't even think to try and rescue them, much less say it out loud."

For as much as I worried about how Rachel and Marshal saw me, or what our life in the big wide world would be like together, I didn't spend a lot of time thinking about anybody else. I guess I seemed pretty daring to somebody like Skywalker.

"How come you never gave me a hard time about my dad?" I asked. "After all the stupid stuff I said about your mom, you could've taken me down a peg or two."

He just shrugged.

"I knew how you felt. And it wouldn't bring either of them back to us."

I nodded in agreement. After that, I stopped calling him Skywalker.

"There wasn't a body to bury," I said. "No way to say goodbye. Dad asked me to move out with him, to start a new life with the nanny, but I couldn't leave Mom behind. Somebody had to stay and try to pull her out of the deep water."

THE LITTLE SEASON

WHEN DAWN CAME, IT BROUGHT A SCARY NEW WORLD WITH IT.
The first thing Cameron and I noticed was there were no bodies.
Scanning the remnants of the FBI's camp from the safety of our
third-floor tower, we couldn't find any trace of the hundreds of
dead agents. Plenty of signs of struggle, but no corpses.

Weirder still, the Fallen had started gutting the government's
makeshift headquarters. Anything that could be carted away
seemed fair game. Lights. Speakers. Hubcaps.

We scanned the camp for Rick and the sheriff's overturned
truck. Several vehicles had been pushed on their sides and at least
two had the doors ripped off their hinges. We had no way of
knowing if they had escaped or died trying. Heck, they could still
be hiding in one of those tin cans for all we could see.

"They got away," Cameron said with a certainty in his voice
that sounded eerily similar to David's when he talked about the
Seven Seals.

"Impressive," I said, not wanting to squash his hopes with a
harsh dose of reality or risk making fun of him with too much
agreement.

Cameron shifted the telescope closer to the church. The Fallen had started pulling apart a storage barn on the outer edge of our property.

"They look like drones," he said, moving away from the telescope to give me a better look. "Like human-sized ants carrying supplies back to some unseen colony."

When I looked through the telescope, what I saw surprised me. Some of the teens sported major injuries and all of them looked disheveled, but there was something else. They didn't look tired or sick or diseased. They seemed profoundly alive. Vibrant. The temperature inside the tower had me shivering, even with a fleece hoodie under my leather jacket. The cold seemed to have no effect on them.

"How far do you think it is from here to the storage barn?" I asked.

"A quarter mile. Maybe a little more. Why?"

"Because they might not pass us by," I said. Cameron was ready to argue the point, but I stopped him. "We don't know what it means, but we should tell David and Liam. They need to know what's happening."

Cameron looked like he still wanted to argue, but to his credit he nodded and followed my lead. We tiptoed back to Liam's office. With the FBI's giant loudspeakers finally silenced, just about everyone had overslept.

I found Rachel right where I left her, curled up in a ball on one side of the leather couch with David slumped on the other side right next to her. Someone had commandeered a blow-up mattress for Marshal and Liam slept with his head down on his desk. The room stank of kerosene from the portable heater. Cameron left the door open to let the fumes dissipate.

I didn't like David sleeping that close to Rachel. He'd taken half a dozen of the church's teenage girls as spiritual wives, citing some Scripture crap. At least, I thought it was crap at the time. Given the current state of the world, I could be wrong about everything.

I brought it up to Rachel once. She said her father would never allow it, and she'd kick him in the "baws" if he ever tried. I couldn't help but smile at the image.

"So what's the word from the eagle's nest?" David asked.

I heard Marshal groan. Liam's back popped in half a dozen places as he sat up. His face had red marks from where he'd slept on his arm.

"Not good," I said. "There are hundreds of them out there, maybe thousands, and they've dragged the FBI agent's bodies off to God knows where."

"What did they look like?" David sat up, took off his glasses, and rubbed his face. "Did they look sick to you?"

"No," Cameron answered. "They looked rapturous."

"Rapturous?" The word caught Marshal's attention. He sat up and gave me the stink eye. At least it looked like the stink eye with half his face covered in gauze and duct tape.

"What are they doing out there?" Liam asked.

"Tearing the FBI camp apart," Cameron replied. "Looks like my uncle and the sheriff got away."

Marshal gave me a skeptical look, but I wasn't about to cast any doubts on Rick's daring escape.

"Most of them are still tearing apart the camp," I added. "But a few have started cannibalizing the storage barn on the edge of our property. They're taking everything, nailed down or not."

"You boys sure you saw them that close to the church?" David asked.

Cameron and I both said yes. Maybe the faint light put out by the kerosene heater played tricks on my eyes, but it looked like David aged ten years in that moment. He let out a long sigh. Whatever counsel he kept in his heart, he didn't share it with us.

"Liam," David said, "I'm afraid our little season will be far shorter than we hoped."

"Should I arrange the dinner?"

I didn't like the finality in Liam's voice. The dinner.

"We should do it tonight, before sundown." David turned to Marshal. "I know you feel like a one-legged man in an ass kicking contest, but I need you to put together three survival packs for me. Light all-weather gear. Try to remember not everyone has your outdoor skills. Cyrus, go with him. And try to learn something."

Marshal started to get up but then stopped himself. "I'm not leaving you. I've seen too much."

"No one said you're going anywhere. I just need you to put together three packs for me. We can talk more about it after dinner."

"What about me?" I asked. "You told me I had to go because I didn't believe. That's not the case anymore. I've seen what's out there and what you can do. I believe."

"I know you do, son. But when the time comes, trust me, you won't." David turned back to Marshal. "Get him set up with the packs before dinner. Cameron can stay here and help me."

Marshal and I headed down the long hall like scolded dogs, our tails tucked between our legs. Having seen what the Fallen had done to the FBI, I didn't want to leave David's protection. We headed to our room first. Marshal took the stairs a lot slower than normal.

"Do you need some help?" I asked.

"I can do it."

"What's the prognosis?"

"Some scarring from the burns. Your mom's not sure about my eye."

"You could lose it?"

He nodded.

"Crap." It's all I could think to say. Now was not exactly the best time to be saddled with a major disability, and we both knew it.

Marshal grabbed a tattered survival guide from the pile of books on his desk. "This one will help you figure out how to find water, what you can and can't eat, how to cover your tracks. There's a bunch of crazy stuff in there about the government taking over and how to start a revolution. Just ignore it."

"Can't I just take food with me?"

"You could, but if those things are even half as fast as they sound, food and water will only weigh you down. Some dried fruit and jerky, a couple liters of water, that's about all you can afford to carry."

"Great. Next you're going to tell me I can't have a gun."

"I guess that's up to you." Marshal grabbed some maps and a "prepper's guide" written by a guy named Cobb. "But you might as well hang a dinner bell around your neck."

"What do you mean?" I followed Marshal upstairs to the tower.

"You saw how they tore apart those speakers and floodlights. You really want to announce your presence to everyone within a square mile? Trust me, you'll be better off with a crossbow and slingshot."

"Come on, a slingshot?"

"Don't laugh. It's quiet and effective. Not to get all biblical on you, but David knew exactly what he was doing when he went after Goliath. It wasn't a plucky underdog story. Plus, you'll never run out of ammo."

"What else?"

"You'll definitely need a med kit. And some flint steel. Flares would make a great distraction, if we can find enough room in the pack. A couple pairs of good socks. Your waterproof boots, of course. A compass and a destination wouldn't hurt."

"Greenbrier," I said without thinking. "Hopefully, Dad's still there. What do I do about the radiation? The FBI seemed really worried about that."

"I don't know." Marshal pulled away the boards that wedged the tower door closed and headed up the steps. "There's some stuff in the Cold War survival book about it."

"I think we should stay together," I said, stopping halfway up the steps. "Splitting up is crap. We should do this together. Like we planned."

"This isn't us running off to get jobs in the city. This is the End of Days, Cyrus. I don't understand why you have to go. I don't want you to go. But what happens now, it's not up to us anymore.

We're in God's hands, which scares the crap out of me. You just have to trust that David knows what he's doing. You said it yourself; he's been right all along. There's a plan. There has to be."

I could tell he had more he wanted to say. Sometimes the most important feelings don't have words. After an awkward pause, Marshal continued up the steps.

"We're going to need the telescope, but you should take the binoculars. They'll be ..."

"What?" I started after him, but he motioned me to stop.

"One of them's on the roof," he whispered. "Make that two— three." His voice went up an octave. "Three of them on the roof."

"Can they see you?"

"I don't know. It's pretty bright outside. I don't think so."

"Back away as slow as you can."

"What if they see me?" Fear froze him to the spot.

"If they come through the window, you can beat them to the door. I'll make sure it closes behind you."

"You sure it's not better if I just stand still?"

"No. It's definitely not."

Marshal took a deep breath and inched his way back down the steps. I followed suit, giving him room to run if the glass shattered upstairs. We made it back to the hallway and closed the door as quietly as we could. Marshal put his full weight against it while I wedged the boards back in place.

At some point, we both remembered to breathe.

PART TEN

Life is a great surprise.
I do not see why death
should not be an even greater one.

Vladimir Nabokov

THE LONG GOODBYE

WE BURST INTO LIAM'S OFFICE, STARTLING RACHEL AWAKE. SHE sat up so fast she fell off the couch.

"They're here!" I yelled. "We saw three of them on the roof!"

"Would you dobbers tone it down!" Rachel pulled herself back on the couch and rubbed the sleep out of her eyes. "You scared the death out of me."

David showed no hint of surprise. He sat on the couch with his eyes closed, muttering a prayer under his breath.

"What are you going to do?" I asked him.

He let out a long breath and then opened his eyes. "We're going to have one last dinner together as a fellowship."

"But—" I groped for the words. I expected him to be alarmed. "You said anyone infected by the Fallen, you said they'd be forever unclean, outside of God's mercy."

"I did." David shifted on the couch. Blood stained the midsection of his rumpled brown shirt. I couldn't help but stare at the ominous blotches. They said more about his limited time on Earth than any sermon.

"So how are we going to save everyone?" I asked.

"You won't be saving everyone, Cyrus. That's my job. Don't

worry. Lucifer will give us our last supper. He's a bastard, but he's not without manners. The Fallen won't breach the church until after nightfall."

Rachel unfolded the jean jacket she'd used as a pillow and put it on over her black sweater. The jacket had flattened her hair on one side and left shallow grooves on her face.

"So what do we do between now and then?" I asked.

"You need to say goodbye. I'll be saving your mom and the rest of the congregation that's willing to follow me. It's time for you to make peace with her."

I just stood there, gobsmacked by the weight of David's words. I trusted his visions now. And I understood why others would do the same. Still, the idea that it was time to say goodbye to my mother ... I'd all but ignored her during the standoff, treating her like the rest of the religious nuts. I opened my mouth to say something, anything, that would make David's words less final, but nothing came out. So I turned and ran out the door.

I found Mom in her bedroom, looking through an overstuffed shoebox.

"Cyrus," she said, "I was just trying to find a few pictures for you. I know you're not going to have room for a lot, but I thought these might help keep your spirits high in the trials to come."

She set aside a handful of four-by-sixes. Her and Dad on their wedding day. My grandparents holding her when she was a little girl. Michael and I at a Yankees game. A picture of her and David after a music festival. Me and Marshal with Rachel on our shoulders.

"I'm sorry I don't have any of your father's parents to give you. I'm afraid he took those with him when he left."

Her voice trailed off. There were photos of Little League and Halloween and Christmases with Grandma and Michael. So many pictures of Michael. My eyes welled up.

"Do you think Dad's okay?" I asked.

"I don't know. Probably not. I promise to look out for you—both of you—once I'm on the other side."

I couldn't sense any anger in her voice, not at my father for trading her in for the nanny, and not at me for staying behind. I wanted to feel the same for her, but she'd said things in anger that could never be taken back, dragged me up and down the country searching for God, and tossed me aside once she found David. And if that wasn't enough, now she was leaving me to clean up the end of the world. What kind of mom does that?

She pulled out a photo of her curled up on a couch, holding a six-month-old version of me. I'd spent the past two years plotting my escape from her. It should be easy to say goodbye. So why did it suddenly feel like I was dying inside?

"This one," she said with tears in her eyes. "This one's my favorite." Her hand trembled as she handed it to me. "You'll always be my sweet face, Cyrus. I know we've had more bad days than good, but I hope you'll look at this picture and remember that it's —that you're my favorite thing in this world."

There was nothing left for me to rage against. Whatever time I thought I needed to create a life of my own and come to terms with her didn't exist. The apocalypse had stolen it. I asked Mom to sit with me and look at the rest of the pictures. I curled up next to her and let her hold me while we did.

When I woke up in her arms, hours later, everyone was getting ready for the big dinner. From the sound of it, bottles of wine had already been opened. Mom chided me for spending too much time with her when I needed to get ready to leave. Then she gave me the longest hug I'd ever had.

"I packed a medical bag for you kids with instructions on how to treat wounds like your ear. Make sure Marshal packs it. If you don't take care of yourself, you could end up with a staph infection."

"Yes, ma'am."

"I love you, Cyrus. Never forget that."

I lingered in the doorway, a handful of pictures clutched tight in my hand. She hadn't said those words in years.

"I never blamed you for Dad," I said.

"I never blamed you for Michael."

She looked down, unable to watch me go. I wanted to hold her, tell her that she had done enough, that it would be okay. With the end so close I finally understood what adults meant when they said there's never enough time.

"I love you, too, Mom." I waited a second. She didn't look up and I don't know if I could have held it together if she had. "I'll see you at dinner."

Walking down the hall, I saw a lot of puffy eyes and red noses, but there was something else. Amid the bustle of preparation and goodbyes, there were smiles. Warm radiant smiles that spoke of a growing tide of anticipation and hope. Maybe even a hint of triumph. David said the end was just the beginning. I could see now, he wasn't just talking about me.

I found Marshal in the kitchen, claiming the remaining stock of beef jerky and hunting in vain for dried fruit. The women had adapted to the lack of power by using a pair of propane camping stoves to cook the food.

"How's it going?" I asked.

"I managed to cram three flares in each pack. They'll make for excellent distractions. Or signals, if anyone's left to mount a rescue."

Marshal always planned for the worst and hoped for the best.

"I still need to find the water purifiers. Odds are nobody's going to be drinking out of a tap any time soon."

Oliver's wife walked through the kitchen in her nicest winter dress, a green and red Christmassy thing with long velvet sleeves that belonged in a Renaissance fair.

"What's up with the dress?" I asked.

"Everyone's gussying up for dinner. The guys put a bunch of tables together on the stage and even scouted up a mishmash of unbroken plates."

"Where's Rachel?"

"Getting dressed up for you, I'd guess. On the run, she's not going to get many chances to wow you." Marshal smiled. "You might think about changing out of that hoodie for her."

"I'll wait until you're done."

"Might be a while. You realize you can't come back for more supplies, right?"

"That reminds me. Mom said she packed us a medical bag. Antibiotics, disinfectant, that sort of thing. She told me to make sure you didn't forget it."

"Yeah, David's been hoarding the entire church's supply for you. I've already divided it up across the three backpacks. Her notes are in your pack."

"Why would he do that?" I asked.

"I guess with the Fourth Seal staring him in the face, he decided you needed it more than he did."

I didn't know what to say. I'd been plotting to lie and poison my way out of Mount Carmel, and all the while David was letting the infection kill him in order to give me a fighting chance. Now I understood why Mom stopped doting over his bandages, and why she believed him to be such a good man.

"You can save that stupefied look for Rachel. Right now, I need your head in the game."

THE LAST SUPPER

THE THIRD WATER PURIFIER TOOK FOREVER TO FIND, BUT Marshal was adamant that each backpack have one. Redundancy's an idiot's best friend, he said with a hint of West Texas charm, as if a grin would cushion the blow of me being the moron in his little scenario. He was full of folksy platitudes that all amounted to a single point. I couldn't count on anything going my way. I had to be prepared to survive alone.

I put on my serious face and tried to throw in some chin boogies to assure him I was taking it all in, but I knew I would never survive alone. I needed Marshal and Rachel more than words could express, and I'd die trying to save them before I would ever face the future alone.

By the time we'd scavenged the last of the supplies, laid every-thing out, and packed it to Marshal's exacting specifications, dinner had kicked into high gear. We could hear laughter, punctu-ated by the occasional cackle, all the way upstairs. More than once, something scrambled across the roof or clawed at a boarded up window in response.

Would David tell us how to get out of here, or would we have to figure it out ourselves? Marshal reminded me that my questions didn't matter right now. I needed to focus on the supplies that my life depended on.

When I thought we were finally done, Marshal dragged me downstairs to Jimmy's old room and raided his climbing bag for some rope and those D-shaped metal rings with spring catches on one side. Marshal called them carabiners. We had just finished cutting lengths of rope for each of the three packs when Rachel showed up in the doorway. She had a full glass of wine in her hand, and judging by the way she sashayed into the room, I'd say it wasn't her first.

"I know you Yanks think it's cool to be fashionably late, but I didn't put on this dress for nothing." She spun in the doorway. Even in the dim lantern light, the light-pink summer dress glowed on her. I almost didn't notice the thermals she had to wear underneath to battle the cold. "It just isn't the same down there without my boys."

"Give us five minutes," I said, knowing it would take at least ten.

She floated back to the dinner and we finished packing. Marshal suggested a quick change of clothes. We hoofed it back to our room, and I tossed on my black suit jacket, normally reserved for weddings, over a white dress shirt. I didn't have time to change out of my jeans or tennies, but I did comb my hair and brush my teeth.

"What about you?" I asked Marshal.

"Suits make me look even fatter." He rummaged through our closet, giggling, and pulled out a striped blue and red tie to go over his sweat-stained t-shirt. Straightening it in the mirror, he tried to pretend the bandage over his eye didn't bother him, but I knew better. He tightened the tie, making a funny richie-rich face, like he was the top hat and monocle guy from Monopoly. "Let's do this."

I've got to admit, dinner kind of surprised me. Far from the somber goodbye I expected, it felt like a celebration. We laughed. We told silly stories about each other. Rachel and I even slow danced. The food, nothing more than pasta and canned sauce, tasted delicious. Looking down the long tables, I realized how much I had grown to care about these people.

I never felt like I belonged at Mount Carmel, but that didn't stop them from treating me like family. Halfway into my second glass of wine, I realized that's what they had become. I'd plotted my escape for years, keeping myself separate, when all I had to do was walk into their arms. The dinner was perfect, almost.

David beckoned us back to his table. He had a smile on his face, but I could tell he was fading fast. I needed to thank him for his sacrifice. The medicine he refused to take would one day save our lives. I wanted to tell him how much my view of the church had changed, how blessed I felt to be with him at the breaking of the world. I started to speak but he motioned for me to take a seat and clinked a butter knife against his half-empty glass of water.

"I can't thank you enough for making the pilgrimage to Mount Carmel," he said, as loud as his threadbare voice could manage. "God gave me a vision and a mission in life, but what I didn't know, what I couldn't imagine, is just how truly blessed I'd be to take this journey with all of you. I am honored to have you with me on the day the Fourth Seal must be broken."

David struggled to his feet, leaning heavily on the long dinner table. I reached for Rachel's hand and held it tight.

"We all knew this day of triumph and sacrifice would come. For most of us, the Merchant's final bargain is at hand and we are destined to fall." He turned his attention to the children. "Don't be scared. The Fifth Seal will pass in the blink of an eye and then the time of our return will be at hand."

I could see the pain on David's face. Infection was ravaging his body, but he refused to bow to it.

"The creatures out there, the Fallen remnants of Babylon, Lucifer has made them forever unclean in the eyes of God. If they were to infect any one of you—"

David's eyes welled up with tears. I looked to Liam and my

mom for some inkling of where David was going with this. The expression on their faces told me neither knew.

"If I let you fight, you will be infected, forever lost to God. If I let you end your own lives, you will be banished from His grace. If I end your lives for you, if I take that sin upon my head, you will all go to heaven."

The room erupted in protest.

"This is not—" The room quieted as David reached for his midsection, grimacing. "We are not going to debate this. Cyrus will be leading a small group on a quest to redeem what's left of this broken world. Anyone brave and willing enough to risk their eternal soul is welcome to join him in this noble pursuit. The rest of you should go to the vault and wait for me."

I looked around the room. The elders, his wives, the kids, the babies ... he couldn't be suggesting that he would murder them to save their souls. Marshal looked equally bewildered, his newfound faith shaken.

"So that's it?" I said before I even realized I had stood up. "You're just going to pile them into the vault and shoot them or something? That's God's grand plan?"

David motioned for me to sit down, but I wouldn't.

"I'll close the vault door for us. The rest is just a question of time and air. The Fallen will not taint my family."

"And what about the rest of the Seals?" I asked. "Do you expect to break them from Hell? 'Cause that's where you're going if you do this."

"Cyrus!" my mother cried out. "How could you! This man saved your life and the lives of—"

"I don't have all the answers, Cyrus. God might not spare me. I don't know. But I'm prepared to sacrifice myself for the souls of everyone here."

"That's great. Just—great!" I turned to face the rest of the congregation. "I don't have a plan from God, and I can't tell you how I'm going to get out of here without the Fallen killing me, but

I will survive. And anybody here that wants to live, now's the time."

Rachel stood immediately. Much to my surprise, so did her father, Liam. Cameron looked like part of him wanted to stand with us, but he couldn't muster the courage and leaned back in his seat.

"So it's Liam and the three amigos," I said to David. "At least one adult recognizes a suicide pact when he hears one. I guess you were wrong about the backpacks. We needed four."

"I'm not going," Marshal said.

The words hung around my neck like a noose. A sense of dread overwhelmed me as I turned Marshal's way and realized he wasn't standing.

"What are you talking about? Of course you're going. You have to ..."

The look on his face said otherwise.

"Why?"

"You said it yourself, Cyrus. All that stuff we thought David imagined. It all came true. And now, at the end of the world, I don't want to leave the only place that ever offered me a real home. I want to stand with David and be resurrected when the Sixth Seal breaks."

"You listen to me, Marshal. Rachel and I are the only reason this place ever felt like home. You can't give up. We need you. Tell him, Rachel."

She didn't say a word. She just reached out and gave him a tearful hug. I couldn't give up that easy, not on Marshal.

"You've got a better shot surviving this than any of us," I said. "For God's sake, you don't need a book to tell you how to survive. You can help people. You can save lives."

"I know what's out there," Marshal said, "and I don't want any part of it."

He tried to give me a hug but I stepped back. There were no words for how betrayed I felt.

"You need to focus," Marshal said. "Your life depends on it now."

I didn't know what to do. I'd never considered the idea of leaving without Marshal. Not before the apocalypse. Not now. I wanted to club him over the head and drag him out of the building, but I knew he could take me in a fight.

The room waited to see what would happen next. Something deep in my heart broke and I rushed forward, hugging Marshal within an inch of his life. There were so many things left to say and no time to say them.

I took a deep breath and let Marshal go.

"Come on," I said to Rachel and Liam. "It's time to get out of here."

I looked back at Mom and David one last time and then headed for the backpacks.

PART ELEVEN

Imagination is more important than knowledge.
For knowledge is limited to all we now know and understand,
while imagination embraces the entire world, and all there ever
will be to know and understand.

Albert Einstein

NO WAY OUT

Taking Marshal's advice, I told Rachel and Liam to dress in layers. We scouted up three waterproof windbreakers to wear over our coats and headed back to my room for the backpacks. Rachel put her pack on quickly, slinging a crossbow over her shoulder. Liam looked at his bow with dread.

"I've never fired one of those before," he said.

"Don't worry about it." I helped him sling it over his backpack. "It's just like a gun."

"I've never fired one of those either."

"Seriously?"

"I'm a barrister, Cyrus, not Dirty Harry."

"Good to know." I smiled like I understood who he was talking about and wrote it off as some weird Scottish thing.

"Rachel's a better shot than me. She'll teach you. Until then—" I lifted mine up to demonstrate, "safety's here. At short range, it's point and shoot. Understand?"

He looked at the bow like it was an unwanted pet Rachel and I had just dragged in from the fields surrounding the church.

"Just try not to shoot us."

I headed down the dim hallway. David had already led everyone into the vault. The air wouldn't last long with the entire church crammed in there. How much time would Mom and Marshal have left? Would it be painful? I needed to focus on staying alive, but it was hard not to imagine them running out of air. I silently cursed David for stealing away my best friend.

"What's the plan?" Rachel asked.

"Pop up to the tower for a quick look around."

"But you said the Fallen were on the roof this morning ..."

"That's right." I took the front steps two at a time. "Why do you think we stopped for the bows?"

We all took a deep breath at the entrance to the tower. Rachel and I covered the door with our bows while Liam quietly removed the beams wedged against it. I cringed as the thick wooden door creaked open. Upstairs, I could hear the sound of blankets rustling against the winter wind.

"Stay here," I whispered to Liam.

It looked like he wanted to protest but was afraid to make a sound. I nodded for Rachel to follow me and headed up the narrow stairs. Halfway, I stopped and held my breath. I couldn't hear anything but the blankets beating against the window sills and the sound of my own racing heart.

When I got to the top, I spun the crossbow around, looking for a target. Two of the three windows were broken and the room had been looted. No telescope. Worse still, no binoculars. At least we were alone.

"What happened?" Rachel whispered.

"They're scavengers," I said, walking up to one of the blankets. "Hopefully, they got what they wanted and moved on."

I used the bow to push aside one of the blankets. The Fallen had carried away almost all of the FBI's camp. The big lights, the speakers, even the cars. There were hundreds of them on the church grounds, carrying away bits of David's crushed Camaro and looting construction equipment near the tunnel. The sun sat low on the horizon, obscuring my view of the smoldering remains of Waco.

"What's it look like on the other side?" I asked.

Rachel tiptoed across the broken glass and pulled aside the far blanket. The intact window shattered before she could open her mouth to scream. I spun around in time to see a redheaded kid, no more than thirteen, diving through the glass at her.

I fired my crossbow quick enough to hit him in the chest. He rolled off Rachel, but the arrow only seemed to make him madder. I rushed him and slammed the stock of my bow into his head.

Rachel scurried past me and we both raced for the stairs. Before I could turn the corner, the kid pounced on me and sent the three of us tumbling down the steps. I heard Liam fire his bow, and for an instant, I was free. I scrambled after Rachel, slamming the thick wooden door closed on the boy.

"Did you hit him?" I asked, half certain I'd just pissed myself.

"Right in the chest." Liam put his weight against the door while we wedged the boards back in place. We could hear the boy flailing around on the other side. "Do you think the door will hold?"

"It's a pretty narrow staircase," I said. "I doubt more than one of them could slam their body into the door at once."

It sounded reassuring, anyway.

"So what are we going to do?" Rachel asked.

"I don't know." I moved away from the door. "There are too many of them out there to chance trying to sneak past."

"I thought you'd have some kind of plan by now." Rachel rested her hands on her hips.

"I do have a plan. It's called not suffocating in the vault."

"Well, that's just—" Rachel let out a squeal as the red-headed monster slammed his body into the door with wild abandon. "Running out of time here."

"You think I don't know that. Liam? Any ideas?"

There was a brief pause and then the teen slammed his body into the door again. This time we heard the sound of wood cracking. I threw my back against the door.

"More boards," Liam said, as he scrambled down the hallway.

Rachel raced to my side. Together we braced the door. The teen stopped pounding and let out a long wailing cry. For a few seconds, he sounded like a baby that just had his favorite toy taken away. Then his voice morphed into something as loud as it was inhuman.

Rachel and I looked at each other.

"I think I liked it better when he was trying to break the door down," she said.

Liam returned with three two-by-fours and a hammer and nails. He dropped the boards on the ground in front of us and we moved away from the door to give him room to work.

"We can't hide here," I said, pacing behind Liam. "And we can't get past the Fallen."

"Thank you, Mister Obvious," Rachel said.

"You're not helping. *Think*. There has to be a way. We can't get away, and we can't keep them out." I stopped pacing. "Wait a minute."

"What?"

"We can't get away. *That's it*. That's the answer."

"What is?"

"We could do it in the gym, but what about the stairs?"

"What are you talking about?" Rachel looked at me like I was crazy.

"Kerosene. There should be plenty of it left. We could use the water storage tanks or maybe even the power lines."

"Have you lost your mind?" Liam asked. "The power's out."

"Exactly," I said. "We've got the carabiners and rope. I think we can do it." I grabbed Rachel and kissed her. "Don't you see? We're not breaking out. We're going to invite them in!"

THE PLAN

I sent Liam after as much kerosene as he could find and headed to Cameron's room with Rachel. I climbed on top of his desk, which was as immaculate as the rest of his room, and popped the ceiling tile, tossing down trash bag after trash bag of fireworks.

"So this is where you guys hid them," Rachel said. "The last place anyone would look."

"You think this is bad? You should see the magazines Cameron has hidden above his bunk."

"Ewww!"

"Why do you think he never ratted us out?" I looked down at the pile of trash bags on the floor. "That's the M-80s and Cats."

I stood on my tippy toes, feeling around for one last bag.

"And now for the most important guest at this party: detonator cord."

"I still don't understand what we're doing."

"Wait for it." I grabbed the bags and headed for the gym. "You're going to love this."

Liam was already there with two five-gallon tanks of kerosene in hand. I crossed the basketball court with Rachel in tow.

"We're going to set up the fireworks in the gym, the chapel, and by the front entrance." I dropped the trash bags on center court. "Liam, I need you to douse all the stairs in kerosene. Start with the back steps, by the cafeteria, and work your way back to us."

He just stood there watching me rip the plastic packaging off a spool of detonator cord.

"I don't have time to explain. You're both just going to have to trust me. Rachel, I need a really big pile of Bibles here and in the center of the chapel." I looked at both of them. "Go!"

I grabbed the detonator cord Marshal and I had hoarded for the better part of a year and ran the length of the basketball court, stopping at a steel ladder attached to the far wall. It led to the catwalk above the gym. After fiddling with the child safety lock, I tucked the spool under my arm and headed up the ladder.

Marshal would have loved this plan. The greatest prank ever. I just wish he was here to see it. Rung by rung, I pulled myself to the top and then jogged down the narrow catwalk, just past the spot where the ATF shot David. I tied off the detonator cord on the handrail and let the spool drop to center court. It landed on one of the trash bags, muffling the impact.

Satisfied with my handiwork, I raced back down the ladder and back to the bag I had pulled the detonator cord out of. I grabbed the palm-sized firing control and stowed it in my back pocket.

Rachel wheeled in a cart towering with Bibles and dumped them in front of me. "You better know what you're doing," she said.

"I need a load twice that size on the chapel stage," I replied.

The sun would be setting soon, and if David was right, we didn't have a lot of time. I ripped pages out of Bibles and stuffed them in paper bags with M-80s, firecrackers, and bottle rockets. The rest of the books got piled around this explosive center in what would eventually look like a ruined pyramid. Before covering the top with hymnals, I cut and stripped the detonator wire, rigging a wad of M80s and Cats into something sure to catch the whole thing on fire. Satisfied with my handiwork, I dropped my little surprise inside.

Stuffing the remaining detonator cord in a trash bag full of fireworks, I headed back up the ladder. After tying off a second detonator cord next to the first, I ran the line along the catwalk and down the steps to the chapel stage. Rachel had run out of Bibles and was ferrying her father's personal library to it. The pile was at least four feet high.

"We need one last pile near the front door," I said to her. She looked at me with exasperation. "Don't worry, I'll take care of that one."

I didn't have enough detonator cord to rig a third run, so I settled for tossing Marshal's books on the kerosene-soaked carpet and dumping the rest of the fireworks on top. I kept *Catcher in the Rye*, I guess because Marshal was always after me to read it. I stuffed the worn paperback in my jacket and took a deep breath. The landing still had bloodstains from when David had saved my life. If he wasn't dead yet, he soon would be. I double-checked the detonator cords, the fireworks, and the kindling. Everything looked set.

Liam and Rachel waited for me in the center of the gymnasium. Both gripped their crossbows like their life depended on them. We could hear the Fallen outside, pulling at boards, howling, probing for a way in.

"This had better be good," Liam said.

"What's the one thing in this gym that works with or without electricity?" I asked.

"What do you mean?"

"This isn't just a church. It's a school, right?"

"Sure."

"So what happens when someone opens the fire doors to the gym?"

"The alarms go off."

"And if there's no power?"

"It's mechanical. The alarm still goes off," Liam replied. "But that would be—"

"Just like ringing the dinner bell?" I smiled. "We get them in the gym and I set off the fireworks from upstairs. We make it so loud and so bright that the Fallen can't help but be drawn in."

"And the kerosene on the steps keeps them from getting to us," Rachel added.

"That's right. While they're tearing the downstairs apart, we slip off to the other side of the church and climb down the water storage tanks. The building will burn for hours, distracting them from our escape."

"Just like the FBI's lights and loudspeakers." I watched Liam think through the plan. "Only they can't shut it off. Nice work, Cyrus."

I couldn't help but smile.

"Who sets off the alarm?" Rachel asked.

"I'll do it," Liam offered before anyone else could volunteer. "I'm rubbish with explosives, and Cyrus needs to be ready to detonate the fireworks."

"Okay," Rachel said, her voice shrinking with fear for her father's safety.

"Rachel and I will wait for you on the catwalk. But kick open that door and haul ass, you hear me?"

I thought Liam might try to scold me for my language, or balk at the way I was ordering him around, but he just nodded. Rachel gave him a quick hug and a kiss on the cheek. The sun was going down and time was short. We climbed the metal ladder and I threaded the cord into the detonator. I turned it on and the battery light flashed green.

I let out a long, deep breath I didn't realize I had been holding. In the back of my mind, I could hear Marshal yelling at me for not thinking to grab an extra set of batteries. "What if the ones in the detonator had gone bad?" he would have said. "You have to plan for everything to go wrong."

"Don't forget to flip the child lock on the trapdoor when you get to the top of the ladder," I yelled down to Liam. "We don't want anything following you up."

He gave me the thumbs up from center court and then lowered his head in prayer. I'd be lying if I said Rachel and I didn't do the same.

PART TWELVE

If it happens that the human race doesn't make it,
then the fact that we were here once will not be altered, that once
upon a time we peopled this astonishing blue planet, and
wondered intelligently at everything about it and the other things
who lived here with us on it, and that we celebrated the beauty of
it in music and art, architecture, literature, and dance, and that
there were times when we approached something godlike in our
abilities and aspirations.

James Howard Kunstler

EXODUS

LIAM KICKED THE GYMNASIUM DOOR OPEN SO HARD IT BOUNCED back and slammed shut, killing the alarm. He pushed it open a second time, wedged a Bible in the door, and ran for the catwalk ladder. The Fallen poured into the gym. Before he could make it halfway to the ladder, I detonated the first batch of fireworks.

M-80 blasts echoed off all four walls. I could feel the explosions in my chest. The crowd of teens turned away from Liam and headed for the pile of Bibles. A whole brick of firecrackers went much faster than I had hoped, followed by the bottle rockets. The Fallen tried to chase after the rockets, but seemed confused when they disappeared with a loud pop.

The gym was half full when the smoldering Bibles finally ignited. The deranged teens circled the pyramid of burning Scripture, mesmerized. None of them seemed to notice us. I handed Rachel my lighter and motioned for her and Liam to head along the catwalk to the stairs that led down to the chapel stage.

I waited until the infected filled the entire gym before triggering the second set of fireworks. The crowd nearest the double doors that connected the gym to the chapel raced in that direction. Rachel ignited the back steps before any of them could think to head upstairs. I caught up to her and Liam and we lit the front steps together.

It took a lot less time than I imagined for the bonfires to choke the upstairs with smoke. Flames danced along the second floor walls where the FBI's tear gas had stained them, accelerating the spread of the fire. We made it to the long hallway, but between us and the water tanks stood a redheaded teenage boy with two arrows in his chest.

He must have broken down the door to the tower. And this time he wasn't alone. Two older teens, covered in dirt and blood, stood beside him. I couldn't tell a lot about them. The thick smoke made it difficult to see and they moved so fast. I raised my crossbow at the outline of the one on the right and then heard someone yell, "Grenade!"

Liam pushed me and Rachel into one of the dorm rooms. The blast threw him against the open doorway, shooting debris into his midsection.

"We don't have a lot of time," I said, picking myself up and heading for the door. "Let's go!"

Rachel looked as disoriented as I felt and Liam's head and chest were bleeding. We scrambled for our crossbows and headed back to the hallway. The grenade had torn a six-foot-wide hole in the floor between us and the water tower. I could see the Fallen burning alive on the first floor, and they could see me.

I looked across the gap to the other side. Marshal stood there waving for me to jump across. *Marshal?* I blinked hard, but he didn't disappear in the smoke.

"Rachel, you go first!" Liam yelled.

She backed up about ten feet and built up a solid run before jumping across. She disappeared in the billowing smoke just after landing past Marshal.

"Now you, Cyrus!"

I could tell Liam was hurt badly and needed my help, but there was no time to argue with him. The smoke burned my lungs in a way that brought back the frantic terror of being gassed by the

FBI. I stooped low, took a deep breath, and then raced for the hole. I didn't look at the other side. I kept my eyes on the uneven floor and threw myself across.

I could hear the floor crack under my weight as I rolled to a stop. I stood up and joined Marshal near the edge. The thick smoke had blackened the bandage covering the right side of his face. I couldn't see Liam at this point, just a tall shadow running toward us. He seemed to stumble on the uneven floor as he leaped. I reached for him, we both did, but I only caught the edge of his hand and then he was gone.

Rachel screamed and went after him, throwing herself headfirst into the burning hole in the floor. I caught her leg and Marshal managed to snag her jacket pocket. Her arm was on fire when we pulled her back up. She screamed for her father and lunged for the hole again. This time we were able to drag her away and pat out the flames traveling up her sleeve. I could barely see Marshal at this point, and I had no idea what happened to my crossbow.

There was no way we were going to make it to the water tanks. The walls were burning all around us, and we were running out of air. I pulled Rachel up the tower steps and yelled for Marshal to follow us. All of the windows had been busted out and a strong breeze gave us our first taste of breathable air. Rachel sobbed uncontrollably.

From the tower, we could see that flames now engulfed the roof over the gym and chapel. The ceiling over the long hallway we had just abandoned was starting to collapse in on itself.

"Marshal, I've got carabiners and rope on the back of my pack."

He grabbed them. From the look on his face, I could tell he knew exactly what I had in mind. I pulled Rachel close while he cut three small lengths of rope and tied them to three hinged metal D-rings.

"There's a steel cable," I screamed to Rachel, "just outside the window. Jimmy used it to run power to the storage barn. I think it's strong enough to carry us one at a time. We're going to ride it down like a zip line!"

Marshal tied the rope to her belt and handed her the spring-clipped metal ring. The burning roof lit up the night sky. Rachel couldn't stop crying.

"Hook the carabiner onto the wire," I yelled. "Gravity will take care of the rest."

"Your first urge is going to be to scream," Marshal added. "Don't do it."

I steadied her as she climbed onto the window ledge. She hooked her line to the steel cable, and I pushed her off.

Marshal handed me a rope and carabiner before climbing out the window.

"I sure am glad to see you," I said.

"Did you think I'd let you have all this fun without me?" He flashed a quick grin and then jumped as soon as Rachel reached the bottom, sliding down the long steel cable.

I tied the rope to my belt as quickly as I could manage and climbed onto the tower's ledge, securing myself to the steel cable. In the instant before I stepped off the tower, I realized that if Marshal was alive, there was a good chance the rest of the church was, too. Would the vault protect them from the fire? Or had my plan of escape doomed them to burn to death? There was no time for answers. I leaped off the ledge and into an uncertain future.

CROSSROADS

WE RAN A GOOD FIVE MILES WITHOUT TALKING. SOMEWHERE along the way, we also ran out of tears. The church burned bright on the horizon, drawing the Fallen from miles away. We came to a dirt crossroads in the middle of nowhere and just collapsed. I pulled Rachel and Marshal close, hugging them as hard as I could.

I didn't have words for what I felt. We had spent so much time scheming to escape our crazy parents. And now that they were gone, we were all alone in a world much more dangerous than we ever imagined.

"I'm sorry," Marshal said. "About your dad. He was a good man."

"I don't think we'd be alive without him," I added.

She wiped her nose on my sleeve and hugged the two of us for a long time. When she finally pulled away, I turned to Marshal.

"What changed your mind?"

"David kicked me out of the vault," he said. "I'm not supposed to talk about it."

I gave him the look, the one that said everybody's dead and gone and it's just us so you better tell me the truth. He looked back in the direction of the fire.

"David told me I was sent to Mount Carmel by God to watch over you. He said the future depended on you surviving, that I needed to protect you. Believe it or not, Skywalker offered to go in my place, but David said it had to be me."

I'm not sure what surprised me more, Cameron's volunteering or Marshal's reluctance. The look on his face told me he believed the decision would cost him his soul.

David had been right about the Seals, the first four anyway. What that meant for our future, I didn't know. Would the Seals continue to break? Would God resurrect David? Would I ever see my mom again?

Hiding behind those questions was one I dared not speak. Were they alive during the fire? According to Kings, the contest of good and evil is decided by a burnt offering. And Daniel said, in the final battle, the last of God's true people would die by sword and flame. Was I part of that plan all along?

If they died in the fire, they died by my hand and not David's. Did I take the sin for David so he could return and break the remaining Seals? And if I did, what did that mean for my soul?

"I don't care why you're here," I finally said. "I'm just glad you are."

"So what do we do?" Rachel asked as she wiped her cold nose. The bitter winds had died down, but the temperature was dropping with nightfall. "Where do we go?"

"North," Marshal said with a certainty that made it sound like the word had been handed down by God himself. Then he offered me a crooked smile. "All my relatives are south. And I don't know about you, but I'm not up for the swim to Rachel's house."

I chuckled and put my head down. It was a small laugh, gone as quickly as it arrived, like a raindrop in the desert. But it was enough to remind me that I would be okay because I had the two of them.

"Greenbrier," I said with a certainty that surprised even me. "We'd be safe there ... even if the Seals are breaking."

Rachel gave me a skeptical look. "I thought you were just

winding me up with those stories about your dad. Isn't he in West Virginia? How the blazes would we even get there?"

"Cars are too loud," Marshal said. "Not to mention the problem we'd have pumping gas without power. And I can't imagine walking."

"Bicycles are quiet," I said. "And fast enough to outrun whatever's chasing us."

Marshal nodded in agreement. Of course, we didn't have bikes, a fact that Rachel was kind enough not to point out.

"As long as I have my boys," she said, wiping away a fresh round of tears, "I don't care where we go."

She stood up, cradling her right arm. The cuff of her windbreaker had melted to her jean jacket and blistered her wrist. She caught me staring and turned away.

"We need to keep moving," she said. "No telling how long that distraction of yours will last."

I wanted to stop and take a look at her arm, but she was right. Mount Carmel would only burn for so long. Marshal fished a compass and knife out of Rachel's backpack and we headed north. My legs ached and my eyes and lungs still burned from the smoke inside the church. That charred smell seemed like it would last for eternity.

I couldn't help but stop for one last look at the distant pyre we had once called home. I wanted more time to think about the things David had said to me. I didn't want to nibble away at the edges, I wanted to solve the puzzle now, but the moon was rising fast, and I knew my time would forever seem short.

The leafless bushes and trees stood silent, like grave markers along the dark gravel road. The three of us walked maybe another three or four miles north. The crisp air kept us alert and jumpy. The lone hoot of an owl, perched on the collapsed remnants of a barn, warned us that danger lurked all around.

The bird's late night call stopped, replaced by the sound of someone racing through bone dry leaves. We dove into a roadside ditch and scrambled to get our weapons ready. Only one bow had survived the escape, but we also had slings and Bowie knives, thanks to Marshal. I held my breath and waited in the cold, dead grass for an attack.

"Crap." Marshal heard a scurrying sound and stood up. "It's just a damn possum. He's probably more scared of us than we are of him."

I exhaled. How long had I been holding my breath? I had a hard time imagining that possum being as scared as us, but then again, the only infected we had seen were teenagers. I stood up and brushed the small bits of hard mud off my jeans.

"How are we going to convince people we aren't infected?" I asked.

"What do you mean?" Marshal stood up and then helped Rachel to her feet. From the look on her face, I'd say she had landed in the ditch on her burnt arm.

"The Fallen, they've all been teenagers. I'm just thinking, when we run into somebody—"

"They might shoot first and ask questions later," Rachel said. "That's going to be a problem."

"Not if we don't put more distance between us and the church." Marshal set a pace for us that my legs wholeheartedly resisted. I kept up for another mile or two, wondering the whole time how a guy his size could run so fast. Just about the time I thought my legs might give out and send me collapsing head first into the gravel, Marshal stopped and crouched on the edge of the road.

I could see another crossroads up ahead, bathed in dim light. Did they still have power here? Maybe the church had been at the outer edge of the blast zone. The source of artificial light hugged the ground, but as we waited and watched, it didn't move or go out.

"Given what you told me about how the Fallen attacked the FBI lights," Marshal said. "I can't imagine they'd let those stand."

"Should we take a look?" Rachel asked.

"I don't know," I said. "Maybe we should go around."

We both looked to Marshal. He was the survivalist, or at least his dad was. He waited a while longer, rubbing his hand along the edges of the duct tape that held his gauze in place. It had to itch like crazy.

"Might be a house on a generator," he said, standing up. "Or maybe an abandoned car. We should at least take a look."

I bit back the urge to protest. Marshal had left David to protect me. He had given up everything to be here for me. The least I could do was trust his survival skills over my own fear.

About halfway to the light, Marshal stopped again and crouched, listening and waiting. No sound. No change in the light. After a few minutes, we continued forward. I had to force myself to loosen my grip on our last crossbow. When I did, color returned to my tingling fingertips.

As we approached the property, it became clear that the light was coming from two sources. A sprawling limestone bungalow, built on a small hill about an acre or so back from the road, had its lights on and curtains drawn. And at the edge of the long gravel driveway, a car had gone off the path and crashed headfirst into a tree.

I put my arm on Marshal's shoulder as a way to get him to stop for a moment and rethink this idea. We could still go around. Avoiding anything bright and shiny seemed like the safer plan to me.

"That's at least a four-bedroom house," Marshal whispered. "If we're lucky, that means kids. And if we're really lucky, that means bicycles."

Marshal brandished his Bowie knife and gave me and Rachel a look that said, get it together. He stood and cautiously walked to the other side of the crossroads. I took a deep breath, looked deep into Rachel's green eyes, and then followed him to the wrecked car.

PART THIRTEEN

Whoever fights monsters
should see to it
that in the process
he does not become a monster.
And when you look long into an abyss,
the abyss also looks into you.

Friedrich Nietzsche

MICHAEL

MARSHAL GUESSED RIGHT ABOUT THE GENERATOR. WE COULD hear it humming from the edge of the road. I started to whisper something about his mad survival skills, but the car's cracked windshield stopped me dead in my tracks. The glass had spider webbed around two head-sized impacts. Bloody handprints dripped from the closed passenger door.

So much for outrunning the Fallen.

My eyes adjusted to the car's dimming headlights, obscuring the darkness between us and the brightly lit house. I followed Marshal around to the open driver-side door, gripping the crossbow tight.

"Jesus," Marshal said, rushing forward. "They're still alive."

I raced to help him, but my attention skipped past the dying parents in the front seat to the hole someone had punched in the back window. I turned and faced the darkness, crossbow ready to fire at the slightest movement or sound.

"Cyrus," Marshal said, "I need your bag."

I slipped it off, motioning for Rachel to join me as I scanned the yard with my bow.

"Anyone else notice the fist-sized hole in the backseat window?" I asked.

Rachel leaned closer to the car, peering into the hole.

"No. Fecking. Way." She stepped back from the car, eyes as wide as saucers. "Some bloke's arm's just laying back there. His whole bloody arm."

The words didn't want to register.

I handed Rachel the crossbow and opened the door. Sure enough, a pale, severed arm, clothed in the torn remnants of a blue flannel shirt, rested on the backseat, right across from an empty baby seat. I scanned the floorboards in the dying light of the car's overhead dome. No baby.

The woman in the front seat tried to whisper something. Her words escaped comprehension in a gurgle of air and blood. From the look of her odd resting place, I'd guess she broke her neck on impact. Her long, dark hair obscured her bloody face.

I looked in Marshal's direction. The guy in the Carhartt jacket was unconscious behind the wheel. His car's head-on collision with the tree had thrust the dash forward, pinning his legs. Judging by the amount of blood pooled under the gas pedal, I'd guess he severed a major artery in his leg. I didn't need my mom here to know he'd die before we could get him anywhere safe. If safe even existed any more.

"Please," the woman in the front seat gurgled, just clear enough for me to make out the word.

I reached over the seat and stroked her matted hair out of her face. She was older but still pretty. I'm not sure she could even feel my hand brushing across her face, but as her eyes lost focus, she managed one last plea.

"Promise ..."

Before I could even think to open my mouth and tell her to hold still or rest her eyes, she was gone. The last wisps of her jagged breath disappeared in the cold air of the apocalypse. She was the second person to die in front of me. The second asking me to promise something. This time I didn't even know what. I closed her eyes and rested my exhausted head on the side of the passenger head rest. It was cold and sticky with what I suddenly realized was drying blood.

I lunged backward, hitting my head on the dome light as I launched myself out of the wrecked car. I landed on my back, scaring Rachel half to death. She spun around and fired the crossbow into the backseat of the car.

"Calm down," Marshal whispered as forcefully as he could manage. "Cyrus just scared himself."

Rachel helped me up. I shivered as I wiped the blood off the side of my face. Then, in an attempt to regain some fraction of my manhood, I crawled into the backseat, past the severed arm, and retrieved the now broken arrow.

"Don't take it hard," Rachel said, reloading the bow. "We can make a new shaft easier than a new tip."

I wanted the blood off my clothes, and I felt stupid for freaking out. What would my mom say, watching me lose it over a little bit of blood on my face?

"How's the dad doing?" Rachel asked.

"Not good," Marshal said. "I don't want to leave him, but I don't think—"

I'm sure in some not-so-deep corner of each of us, we wanted this guy to pull through, to be the adult we lost when Rachel's dad died. But that wasn't going to happen.

"We can't help him," I said, making the decision for the group. "We're wasting too much time here. We need to move on."

Marshal nodded and then, after a short prayer, stepped back from the driver's side door. The man's upper body slumped without Marshal's support and his arm dangled, revealing an old-school silver wristwatch, the kind you have to wind up. It looked out of place with his worn jacket and faded blue jeans.

Marshal zipped up my backpack and slung it over his shoulder, turning my way. "What now?"

"Check the house for supplies and then get the heck out of here."

Marshal shut off the car's headlights, and the three of us turned toward the sprawling limestone bungalow. The glow of the distant house did little to illuminate the darkness that surrounded us or calm our fears. Each step I took felt more reluctant than the last, like my body was trying to tell me that searching this place was a terrible mistake.

About halfway up the drive, I stumbled over a black metal bat, hidden in the darkness along the edge of the overgrown yard. The dark aluminum clanked across the gravel driveway. We froze on instinct. Listening. Waiting. Praying.

Nothing happened.

I tucked my knife away, took a few steps forward, and picked up the bat, tightening my hands around the cool rubber grip. I already felt safer. It was a home run derby special. The double-walled aluminum shone through the worn black paint along the bat's edge and sweet spot. I took a check swing and could almost hear the clank of the ball as it sailed over Mount Carmel. Resting it on my shoulder, I tried not to think about the fact that the church didn't exist anymore.

Marshal was also right about the kids. The whole yard turned out to be a minefield of abandoned toys. Some of them glinted in the eerie glow of the house. Others hid like sharks in the tall, dead grass, waiting to take a bite out of our ankles. We took it slow, careful not to make any noise that could be heard over the sound of the house's emergency generator.

I stopped at the base of the front steps. Someone—make that something—had ripped the screen door right off its hinges and hurled it onto the front lawn. Did I really want to face off with a creature that could do something like that? I gripped the bat tighter and took a step forward, ready for some horror-movie monster to jump out and attack me. Marshal and Rachel followed close behind, equally tense.

I climbed the steps slow, trying to take in every sound, every movement. I had to be ready to strike. From the porch, I could hear the sound of a television, but how could that be? There were no stations left to watch. The front door had been left open. Who in their right mind leaves their door open to the apocalypse? I needed to stop asking questions I didn't want the answers to.

I pushed the red front door all the way open and walked into a dirty but well-lit mudroom. Boots and winter coats had been knocked over in a mad dash to get out of the house. I stepped over them and moved toward the second door. Warm air, so wonderful it almost brought tears to my eyes, billowed out of the next room, along with the sound of ... *Sesame Street?*

One half-open door was all that separated me from the answer to this strange riddle. I took a deep breath and pushed it open, stepping into a living room that so defied logic, I just about dropped the baseball bat.

A grubby, one-armed teenager, clearly infected, sat across the living room on a leather recliner with a baby in a sling across his chest. He was muttering something to the baby that sounded like a garbled version of "Sunny Days" as he tried to feed the little one a jar of baby food.

His arm, no doubt sitting in the backseat of the car outside, protruded from his torn plaid shirt in a gnarled stump. I didn't know a tenth as much about medicine as my mom, but I knew enough to be certain that he should have bled out, not healed.

To add to the insanity of the moment, the family had filled the warm, bright room with birthday balloons and a handmade sign that said, "Happy 1st Birthday, Michael!" in red, blue, and green letters. I took a step into the room and tightened my grip on the bat. The teenage boy seemed so focused on the baby that he didn't notice us.

It wasn't until I took a second step forward, putting my body between the baby and the TV, that the little one cried out and I caught his attention. The teen's head snapped up, his eyes squinting at the three of us. I froze.

"We're not here to hurt anyone," I said. "We're just passing through."

He didn't respond.

I started to back away. The moment I moved, he dropped the baby food and lunged at me. In the instant it took him to cross the living room, mouth opening to bite me, nails ready to claw my face off, I pulled back the bat and took a swing that would determine whether I lived or died.

HOME RUN

IF I LIVE TO BE ONE HUNDRED, I WILL ALWAYS REMEMBER THE hollow clank of that bat's sweet spot as it crushed the side of his face. It caught him just under his cheekbone on its way up and across his skull. I felt a rush of hot, ragged breath and a splatter of blood across my face as the bat shattered every bone in his deranged head, sending him sideways over a glass coffee table to crumple in a heap on the other side of his family's dark leather couch.

I rushed forward, not to finish him off, but to rescue the baby now being suffocated under the weight of his chest. The muffled wails became piercing as I rolled the lifeless teenage body over. I had to force myself not to vomit as the impact of my swing became clear. He died with his arms around the baby. His last impulse, as near as I could imagine it, was to protect little Michael.

A dark halo of blood now framed the infected teen's mangled head. I wrestled the baby out of its sling and unzipped my black leather coat, holding the little boy close to my chest. It didn't help quiet his cries. Marshal slammed the front door shut, throwing his body against it to block what I'm sure he imagined to be an onslaught of infected, all while The Count sang about the number of the day in the background.

My eyes turned to the wall of pictures behind the couch. The parent's wedding photo was there, alongside pictures of their children growing up. From the look of it, they had a son, two teen daughters, and the late-life surprise I held in my hands. I couldn't help but notice a picture of the boy, dead at my feet, in his Little League uniform. He was smiling as he pretended to hit a home run.

Stepping back from the expanding pool of blood, I couldn't help but replay the moment of impact in my head. I didn't even have time to think about what to do. I just—I turned to the television. How could the Fallen understand anything about a videotape? He would have had to rewind it and hit play over and over again.

"Why would he feed the baby?" I finally muttered out loud. "Why not just kill it like they're killing everything else, like he would have killed me?"

No one had an answer.

Looking back at the blood-soaked heap in the corner, I wanted to throw up. I didn't feel like a hero, slaying a monster and saving a baby. I felt like a murderer. I think he would have killed me, but that didn't take away the sound of the bat crushing the life out of him, or the fact that he died trying to save his little brother from me.

"Cyrus!" Marshal screamed.

I turned just in time to see Rachel fire an arrow past my head. I actually heard the thing sail past my good ear. The smart thing would have been to turn and take another swing, but my first reaction was to duck and protect the baby. I heard a body fall to the ground behind me. I turned to face a teenage girl with long, black hair writhing in pain on the kitchen floor, just short of the living room. She was trying to pull the arrow out of her eye socket.

I recognized her from a senior photo on the wall over the couch. In the picture, she looked a little like Rachel, with much bigger, teased-out hair. Her jean jacket might have been the exact same.

Marshal crossed the room and grabbed the bat out of my hands. He raised it to within an inch of the ceiling and brought it down hard on the girl's head, blood sprayed all over his jeans.

"There should be one more," I said, pointing to the wall of photos behind the couch. Marshal took a step into the kitchen, bat ready.

"Nope," Rachel said, stepping closer to the wall of photos. "Too old to be living at home."

"You sure?" I asked.

"Look at the picture on the bottom left. You think Daddy's going to let his little princess show off those chebs while she lives under his roof?"

I took a closer look. The girl in the photo had pulled her white Florida State tank top tight enough to expose the top of her black push-up bra. Her eyes, partially hidden behind a pair of reflective aviators, lingered on the photographer with a hint of mischief that her girlfriends in the photo seemed to share. Sorority sisters from the look of it, the kind you'd find in one of Cameron's *Playboys*.

Rachel elbowed me in the side for taking a little too much time to examine the photo and pointed to a younger one, the photo I'd noticed with the two sisters. I went back to the tank top photo. Another girl had on a college t-shirt.

"Florida State," I said to Marshal. "Rachel's right. She's off at college. Probably too old to be infected, anyway."

I was guessing about that last part. When nothing makes sense, you start looking for rules and rationales, boundaries to explain the status quo. Teenagers were the real threat, I told myself. That limited our enemies but also made us prime candidates to join their insanity.

Rachel had already reloaded her bow. I could tell she was trying to work up the courage to retrieve the arrow that saved my life. At least the baby had calmed down and was sucking his thumb in the comfort of my thick jacket lining.

"The warm air's nice," Marshal said. "But we shouldn't stay. I'm going to check the garage for bikes."

"Sounds good," I said. "We'll scavenge the bedrooms, find some baby clothes."

"What are you talking about?" Marshal asked.

"The kid's going to need clothes."

"Cyrus, you can't take that thing with us. He'll get us all killed."

"Thing? His name's Michael," I said, gesturing to the balloons and streamers above Marshal's head. "We can't just leave him here to die."

"So what are you going to do for milk, drag a fricking cow around on a rope?" Marshal's hands gripped the bat. It almost looked like he wanted to take a swing at me. "Look, I know it's not easy, but we're lucky to have fought off two of those things. One yelp from a baby at the wrong time, and we could be staring down a hundred."

"I won't do it," I said, turning back to Rachel for support. "I won't leave him."

She looked like she didn't know which side to pick, crazy or monstrous. I held the baby close to my chest, comforting him. He had more than just my brother's name. He had his eyes. Deep blue eyes that reminded me of the ocean.

"This isn't a vote," I said. "I'm not leaving Michael. Period. If that means I'm on my own, if you two don't want to stomach the risk, I—I won't fault you for it. I love you both, but I can't leave a defenseless baby to die. It's not right."

Marshal walked away from me and headed into the kitchen, muttering something under his breath. Just before he got to the sink, he spun around with the bat and took out his frustration on one of the kitchen cabinets. Cheap plates and mismatched coffee mugs crashed to the hard-tiled floor, startling Rachel. When he looked back my way, I could see he wanted to throttle me, but I stood my ground.

"The world has to be more than every man for himself," I said. "We just killed the last of this kid's family. It might be the dumbest decision in the world from a survival standpoint, but we have a responsibility to him."

"And what are you going to do when we find the next one, and the one after that? Are we going to start a traveling daycare?" Marshal looked Rachel's way. "You okay with this insanity?"

She didn't reply.

"Fine," Marshal said. "But if I get killed because of this little bastard, I'm going to haunt you both for eternity. You hear me?"

"I'll check the bathroom for medicine," Rachel said, moving away from the dead girl on the floor with the arrow still sticking out of her eye socket. Marshal gave me one last glare of disapproval before heading for the garage.

And just like that, I went from being a scared teenage survivor to a terrified father. I didn't feel like I was ready to be either, but the Universe rarely waits until you're ready. The answers, as David taught me, come in God's time, not your own.

PART FOURTEEN

Ours is essentially a tragic age,
so we refuse to take it tragically.
The cataclysm has happened,
we are among the ruins,
we start to build up new little habits,
to have new little hopes.
It is rather hard work;
there is now no smooth road into the future:
but we go round,
or scramble over the obstacles.
We've got to live,
no matter how many skies have fallen.

D.H. Lawrence

SHELTER FROM THE STORM

RACHEL WAVED ME INTO THE BATHROOM LONG ENOUGH TO WIPE the blood off my face. I tried to avoid the mirror and any thoughts about the origin of the red stains on her washrag. The Fallen hadn't laid a hand on me, but I was wearing their blood and the inside of my leather jacket was stained from carrying little Michael around. Was I forever unclean in the eyes of God? Was Michael? How could any of us know?

It had taken me five months of playing dive bars in David's band to save up for my leather jacket. I had tried on at least twenty before I settled on this one, and now it was ruined. I felt like the biggest jerk in the world for getting upset about the bloodstains. I mean, the kid just lost his whole family, but it was the coolest thing I ever owned, and I bought it myself.

We grabbed children's ibuprofen and a half used Z-Pak out of the medicine cabinet, leaving the rest. Michael's nursery was twice as large as my dorm room back at Mount Carmel. Next to the crib and changing table sat an ornately carved rocking chair and a small mountain of stuffed toys. The room was *Sesame Street* themed, with a plush version of every character peeking out of some corner.

Rachel crammed cloth diapers into her already overstuffed

backpack while I searched the closet for another baby sling. No way I was taking the blood-soaked one off Michael's older brother.

"Should we tell him he's ours?" Rachel asked. "If he lives long enough to ask, I mean."

"Why would we do that?"

"To spare him the pain of the truth. You never talk about your brother, but that doesn't mean I don't know how much him being gone bothers you." She grabbed little Michael from me and sat him on the changing table. "If you had been his age, your parents might have hidden it from you."

I gave up on the closet and moved on to a nearby clothes hamper, pulling a baby sling out of the bin that looked brand new. As I slipped my leather jacket off, my gaze drifted up to a picture on the wall. The whole family surrounded mom and newborn Michael in the hospital.

"Would you have wanted your father to lie to you about your mom?" I don't know why I asked the question. I already knew the answer. "If either of our parents had pretended it didn't happen, we wouldn't be together."

I pulled the picture off the wall and took it out of the frame, folding it up and tucking it in a little Ziploc bag with my own pictures.

"We didn't know it back then," I said, "but your mom and my brother ... they saved us. They helped us find each other. Without them, we might not be alive."

"Good news. Strange news."

Rachel yelped at the sound of Marshal's voice.

"I could use some good news," I said. Marshal's face beamed with excitement. I couldn't imagine news good enough for that smile.

"Four mountain bikes in the garage. One even has a little covered trailer for the kid."

"That is good news," I said, looking at him like he was a Martian. His goofy grin seemed ready to explode.

"And the strange?" Rachel asked.

"I think we just won the apocalypse lottery."

I waited for an explanation, or at least a punchline. Marshal didn't give me either.

"I don't get it," I finally said.

"You will. Come on, princess."

I put my leather jacket on over the sling and took the freshly changed and clothed Michael back from Rachel. After a few seconds of tightening and testing, I grabbed my bat from Marshal and followed him through the living room and kitchen.

He opened the door to the garage with a grand flourish and even said "ta-da" as we walked through the doorway. The overhead light dimly illuminated the mostly empty space. My eyes were immediately drawn to the peg-board wall on the far side. It held a vast array of wood-working tools: chisels, saws, hammers, hand axes, and even a rusty scythe that looked like it came straight out of a horror movie. I couldn't help but imagine how badass I'd look wielding that long curved blade against the Fallen. Of course, the practical value of a weapon like that was less than zero.

The bicycles were there, along with an attachable cart for little Michael. Apart from that, a drill press and table saw. Nothing to warrant Marshal's level of glee.

"I still don't get it."

"Look behind the table saw."

If Marshal hadn't mentioned it, my eyes would have skipped past the fact that the table saw and drill press stood a good three feet away from the back wall. Behind them, a concrete stairway led somewhere under the garage.

"This house is old enough to have been built during the Cold War," Marshal said. "At the bottom of those steps is a big metal door with a bomb shelter sign on it."

Marshal trembled with excitement.

"Think about it. An honest to God bomb shelter. Food and supplies and a safe place to rest. We could make a home of it, wait out the apocalypse."

"Have you gone down there?" Rachel asked.

"Do I look stupid enough to open an underground door without backup?"

"You really want me to answer that?" she said with a smile.

The idea of a safe place to call home was infectious. Even I had a grin on my face as we walked over to the steps.

"The kid wouldn't be a problem," Marshal said. "Think about what David told you about rebuilding the world. We could hunker down here and wait the Fallen out. It's not like they can go on forever. The virus has to have a lifespan."

More made-up rules to explain things we didn't understand.

My legs desperately wanted a safe place to collapse. I looked down the steps at our lottery ticket. Marshal produced a flashlight from his pack and shined it on the rusty, oversized door. I looked at the fallout shelter sign like a starving man looks at an all-you-can-eat buffet.

"Why wouldn't the family hide here?" Rachel asked. "Why try to escape in the car?"

"Maybe they didn't have time to think it through," I said. "Your teens go homicidal. You grab the baby and run for it."

"Yeah." Rachel grabbed the flashlight out of Marshal's hand. "That sounds about right."

"What are you doing?" Marshal asked.

"Having a go." She could tell he was going to object. "You can stuff the chivalry back in your pants, Marshal. I'm not your damsel in distress."

She handed Marshal the bow and pulled out her Bowie knife.

"Something jumps out at me, you shoot first and worry about hitting me later."

"Got it."

She hesitated.

"Try not to sound so enthusiastic about the idea."

I followed Rachel halfway down the steps, ready to pounce on anything that jumped out at her. I don't know if little Michael could somehow sense danger, but he didn't let out a peep.

Rachel gripped the thick metal door handle. It turned easy

enough. But, no matter how hard she pulled, the door didn't budge.

"Locked?" I asked. "Or rusted shut?"

Rachel surveyed the rusty door with her flashlight.

"Maybe both," she said. "Marshal, see if there's a crowbar up there."

After a few minutes of fumbling in the dim light of the garage, Marshal returned with a crowbar. I reached up for it and then took a step toward the door before realizing how difficult it would be to use a crowbar with a baby strapped to your chest. To her credit, Rachel didn't say anything snarky. She just reached for the crowbar and wedged it between the door and the surrounding concrete.

She put her weight into it, but the door wouldn't budge. Bits of concrete crumbled along the edge of the crowbar, but not enough to shake loose the rust. Marshal squeezed past me to help her. None of us wanted to contemplate the idea that the shelter was locked. The possibility of a safe house had been dangled in front of us, and we weren't about to entertain any scenario that required us to let go of it.

After a couple of unsuccessful tries, my mind started to return to the bikes and the fact that we had a limited window of distraction to escape. Mount Carmel wouldn't burn forever. I started to say something, but the door let out a loud creak and budged a few inches.

"Let's see if we can rock it back and forth," Marshal said. The two of them pushed it close and pried it open a couple more times. With each attempt, the rusty hinges groaned and gave a little more. The door was about a foot and a half open when Rachel decided to take a peek.

"It's cozy," she said, leaning in with the flashlight. "Like a little studio apartment. Lots of dust and must."

She leaned back out, pointing the flashlight our way.

"Come on, boys. Let's check out our new flat."

HOME

WE FOLLOWED RACHEL INTO THE SHELTER. HER FLASHLIGHT bounced past the small living room-slash-kitchen to the four bunks chained to the curved sidewalls. Past the beds, floor-to-ceiling shelves lined the back wall. Everything was covered in plastic tarps and a healthy layer of dust. Thankfully, none of us had serious allergy problems.

I heard Marshal flick a bank of switches behind me. Two of the four overhead lights flickered for a minute and then actually came to life. The concrete ceiling hung low, borderline oppressive, at maybe six feet high. It curved down to meet the floor, forming a cramped semi-circle of living space. Despite the odd shape, it was about the size of a studio apartment, close to what we could have afforded in Austin if the apocalypse hadn't derailed our plans.

"It's a fixer-upper for sure." Marshal pulled the plastic off the ancient TV-stereo combo, stirring a small cloud of dust. "But not without its vintage charms. I can't say I'm a fan of the whole no-window look."

I turned to the plastic-covered couch. My legs begged me to unzip the cover and collapse. Marshal turned the radio on and traveled up and down the dial. Nothing.

"Boys, check this out." Rachel reached for a switch above the kitchenette's mini-sink. Light flickered behind a fake window, illuminating a yellowed picture of a well-manicured backyard.

Marshal looked out the fake window and smiled. "I call dibs on mowing the lawn. You two can argue over the other chores."

I walked over and turned the faucet on. We heard a pump under the sink chug for a few seconds before brown water poured out. It had a strong sulfur smell that caused little Michael to shudder in his sling.

"That's disgusting," Rachel said.

"But drinkable with a filter," Marshal replied. He pointed to the toilet next to the sink. "If we've got water pressure to the sink, I bet we've got a working toilet."

Rachel looked the open air commode up and down, grimacing at the lack of privacy. I could almost see the inner dialogue going on in her head as she realized that life on the run wouldn't offer much better. She popped open the lid.

"Empty."

"I bet they just have the water lines turned off," I said. "Nobody wants standing water for—however long this place has been here."

I followed Marshal past the bunks to the wall of supplies along the back of the shelter.

"1950s," Marshal said, "if I had to guess by the TV."

He pulled the plastic off of the shelves and started looking at the canned food.

"Hey, Cyrus. How do you feel about peaches that expired in 1962?"

I didn't know how long canned fruit could last, but I was pretty sure I didn't want to chance eating something grown around the time of the Cuban Missile Crisis.

"You know how you boys are always saying Twinkies never go bad?" Rachel pulled something out of the kitchen cabinets, a bloated greenish-brown blob wrapped in plastic. "I'm pretty sure they do."

"So food's going to be a problem," Marshal said, "but we can scavenge what they have left upstairs, maybe even hit up a few of the surrounding houses. We could cram a good three or four months of food down here."

"You think that'll be enough?" I asked.

"No idea, but it's got to be better than making a run for it."

We didn't take a vote. We all nodded, and without a word of debate, this became home. Our first home together, as grownups. Not the one we had planned, but nothing short of a miracle, given the state of the world around us.

"We should grab the bikes," I said. "Store them down here. They'll be gone for sure if the Fallen come this way."

Marshal gave me an almost parental smile.

"Let's get the food down here before my legs give out," I said. "My body wants to sleep for a week."

"Good luck with that." Rachel pointed to the little boy hanging from the sling across my chest. "You're on changing and feeding duty starting now."

We headed for the door. I stopped at a couple of metal lockers crammed along the front wall and opened one on a whim. Thin white jumpsuits hung from wire hangers. On the shelf above them were some old maps and a bunch of red clip-on badges that said "Nuclear Chicago" on the front. I grabbed one. The badge was date stamped 8-24-59.

"No!" Marshal yelled. I dropped the badge, reached for my knife, and turned his way. He was just standing there, staring at the shelter's door. "No. No. No."

"What is it?" Rachel asked.

All Marshal did was keep muttering the same word.

I walked up to him, but he acted like I wasn't even there. Tears streamed down his cheeks.

"What the heck, Marshal?"

"No locks," he said, kicking the door. "Somebody got rid of the damn locks."

I looked at the side of the metal door and sure enough, the

spot that should have held an oversized deadbolt or a reinforced steel bar or something, *anything*, was missing.

"No wonder they didn't hide out here," Rachel said. "They knew they couldn't lock themselves in."

"Maybe we could shore it up," I offered. "Barricade the door like we did at Mount Carmel."

"We nailed, what, five two-by-fours to that tower door?" Marshal pulled back his fist like he wanted to punch the concrete wall. "They still busted through."

"What about putting something heavy in front of it?" Rachel asked. "Or camouflaging the entrance."

"Risky." Marshal looked my way. "What do you think?"

Every bit of my heart and soul wanted to stay, to call this place home and work toward building a life here, but I couldn't help but feel like we would be trading one deathtrap for another.

"Mount Carmel had a bunch of escape routes and we barely made it out alive," I said. "This place only has one. The way the Fallen tore apart that FBI camp, they'd find us for sure, and we'd have nowhere left to hide."

Marshal wiped away his tears but couldn't stop crying. I had to look away before I started. You'd think, after all we'd been through, that a setback like this wouldn't hit us so hard, but it did. This was our lottery ticket. Our miracle. Our home.

My mind drifted back to the car wrecked outside and the woman in the passenger seat. I looked down at little Michael. He sucked his thumb, ignorant of the dangerous world around him. It didn't take a rocket scientist to figure out what his mom wanted me to promise.

"It wasn't going to be anything but a temporary solution," I said, putting my arm on Marshal's shoulder. "Now. Three months from now, we were still going to have to face the other side of that door."

I reached for Rachel and she joined us in a group hug.

"The three of us," I said. "We're home. Not Mount Carmel. Not this place. Not even Greenbrier. Us. Together. Understand?"

Marshal nodded and wiped away his tears.

"Promise," I said. "Forever."

Rachel gave us both a peck on the cheek, fighting back her own tears. "You'll always be my boys."

"Yeah," Marshal said, pulling us even closer. "I promise."

POINTS OF DEPARTURE

I'D LIKE TO SAY WE HAD MORE THAN THAT BRIEF MOMENT TO sort things out, but the apocalypse had other plans for us. We needed to get moving. "The government could still contain this thing," I reminded them. "Which means we need to get out of the infected zone before they lock it down."

"Fair play," Rachel said, looking back at the shelter. "We should probably give the place a quick once over, see if we can find anything useful."

I'm not sure what Rachel was hoping to discover in this freeze-dried tribute to the Cold War, but Marshal agreed and we took a few minutes to search the place. I popped open an old military footlocker that doubled as a coffee table for the couch, but it was full of old magazines and musty comic book versions of classic literature. Marshal and Rachel came up empty-handed, too.

It wasn't until we headed for the door that Marshal stopped at the locker with the white jumpsuits.

"You think those radiation badges are still good?" I asked.

"No," Marshal said, pulling out one of the old maps I had skipped past. He unfolded it. "But this. This could be the difference between life and death."

I stopped with one foot out the door. Now that we had decided against staying, the clock in my head was ticking.

"Those maps are older than all of us put together," I said. "What good could they possibly—"

"See these symbols?" Marshal held the map up to the light. The folds were so crisp I doubted anyone before us had ever bothered to unfold it. "If they mean what I think they mean, this is a map of fallout shelters across Texas."

"Would they still be around?" Rachel asked.

"Schools and government buildings." Marshal looked my way. "The kinds of places you don't tear down when they get old."

"We could use them like safe houses," I said. "Make our way out of Texas."

It was enough to give us hope.

Marshal grabbed the maps and we threw as many supplies as we could into the baby trailer. Rachel changed Michael a second time, and I used some spray paint to leave a message on the rusted shelter door.

NO LOCK! NOT SAFE!

It might save someone else the time we spent here. Without the maps, the shelter was nothing more than an underground death trap.

"You sure this Greenbrier place is real?" Rachel asked. "It's not some tall tale your dad conjured up to impress you?"

"My dad's a lot of things," I said, hopping on my mountain bike. "But he's not a liar. You'll see."

Marshal opened the garage door and we headed back down the gravel driveway. Much to our relief, peddling used an entirely different set of leg muscles than running. I stopped at the wrecked car and grabbed the watch that had looked so out of place on the dad's wrist. I'd give it to Michael when he was old enough. Looking at the parents one last time, I put my hand on their little one's head.

"I promise."

We peddled away from the house in silence. I couldn't help but feel like we were leaving the last of our old lives behind. Would we make it out of Texas? Would we make it to tomorrow? There were no easy answers, and no adults to show us the way. In the end, we didn't have much of a plan. Just some old maps, a little luck, and each other. For us, the end of the world really was the beginning.

ACKNOWLEDGMENTS

Writing is often a solitary art, but no book is formed in a vacuum. This is true of the debut novel more than any other. The book you now hold in your hand grew out of countless late night conversations with Doug Fivecoat, Kyle Hendrix, and Jill Gordon. These wonderful people did more than just help me write a first novel. They helped me dream myself into being a writer.

This book exists because Maurice Broaddus and Jason Sizemore took a chance on a writer of modest credits, because Geoffrey Girard and Jennifer McGowan pushed me to turn this crazy idea into a novel, because Sara Larson and Rodney Carlstrom infected me with their limitless enthusiasm for my work. I hope each of you knows that your writing and your friendship shaped every page.

Finally, I'd like to thank Daniel and Trista Robichaud for dropping everything to read (and reread) this book, Lesley Conner for moving heaven and earth to get it ready for the 25th anniversary of the standoff, and my parents and grandparents for always encouraging me to dream.

ABOUT THE AUTHOR

Jerry Gordon is the Bram Stoker Award-nominated co-editor of the *Dark Faith*, *Invocations*, and *Streets of Shadows* anthologies. His short fiction has appeared in numerous venues including *Apex Magazine* and *Shroud*. When he's not writing and editing, he runs a software company, teaches, and longs for a good night's sleep. You can find him blurring genre lines at www.jerrygordon.net.

 facebook.com/jerrygordon

twitter.com/jerrylgordon

Made in the USA
Lexington, KY
01 May 2018